A BILLIONAIRE'S

Infatuation

A BILLIONAIRE'S

Infatuation

LOVE AND WEALTH
Book One

USA Today Bestselling Author
Tamika Brown Writing As

MIKA B.

A Billionaire's Infatuation
Paperback Edition
Copyright © 2026 by Mika B.

Love N. Books Press
An Imprint of Wolfpack Publishing
1707 E. Diana Street
Tampa, FL 33610

www.lovenbookspress.com

All rights reserved. No part of this book may be reproduced in any form or by any electronic or mechanical means, including information storage and retrieval systems, without express written permission from the publisher, except for the use of brief quotations in reviews. Any use of this publication to train generative artificial intelligence (AI) technologies is expressly prohibited.

This book is a work of fiction. References to historical events, real people, or real places are used fictitiously. Any similarity to real persons, living or dead, is purely coincidental and not intended by the author.

All brand names and product names used in this book are trademarks, registered trademarks, or trade names of their respective holders. Wolfpack Publishing is not associated with any product or vendor in this book.

Edited by My Brother's Editor

A Billionaire's Infatuation was originally self-published in 2020 by Mika B.

Paperback ISBN 978-1-969876-24-0
Ebook ISBN 978-1-969876-23-3
LCCN

A BILLIONAIRE'S *Infatuation*

CHAPTER ONE

"Shit, I'm gonna be late." I swore as I stepped up to the counter and placed the same order I have for the past four years. A white chocolate caramel mocha for me and a large, black coffee for my asshole of a boss. I handed my debit card to the barista to pay for both. Eight dollars and fifty-six cents, five days a week and sometimes six (depending on what we were working on), really added up, especially when you're broke.

I checked my watch one more time. I hated being late for work in the morning, even more so because I knew he would be a dick for at least half of the working day because of it. My name is Remi McMillan, the personal assistant to one of the wealthiest businessmen in New York City. The founder and CEO of St. Clair Technologies. *Tony St. Clair.* One of the finest and sexiest men I'd ever seen in my thirty-two years of life. Also, one of the world's most eligible bachelors and the bane of my existence.

Finally grabbing my order, I booked my way down the busy sidewalk two blocks to the St. Clair Building. The fifteen-story building was at the center of one of the busiest intersections in the city. I reached the revolving door five minutes after eight.

More than likely, he'd be sitting behind his mahogany desk, looking at his expensive watch, and waiting to bust me for being late.

I rushed across the lobby to the elevator. "Great, it's on the top floor," I muttered, smashing the first-floor button repeatedly as if it would make it quicken its pace.

Mercilessly, the elevator made its descent. I switched my weight from foot to foot, back and forth, waiting impatiently for the doors to open so I could step in and get my workday underway. Relief swept through me as the doors revealed emptiness. I checked the time again as the *ding* indicating my floor reverberated around me. The one-minute ride felt more like an hour.

While balancing the two cups of coffee, I sprinted out of the elevator and hurried toward my office. I flung the door open and unceremoniously dropped my bag on the floor next to my desk. I threw my empty cup into the trash can, scooped a planner from my desk, and rushed to the double doors at the end of the hall. Pausing for a few seconds to gather myself, I took two deep breaths before knocking softly on the door. I learned my lesson the first day about entering his office without knocking first.

I will never forget how his soft, caramel-colored eyes caught mine as I stared, horrified at him fucking a woman sprawled across his desk. She never flinched as he continued to pound in and out of her. And my boss? There was a playfulness behind his brown orbs as he locked eyes with me, almost as if he wanted me to watch. I couldn't move from the sheer shock of it all. But I didn't dare look away for fear he would punish me somehow…

Intense. *That was the only way I could describe the look he gave me. A few minutes later, his movements became jerky. He grabbed the woman's hips and roared, or it sounded like a roar to me. I'd never heard a man sound like that as he released his seed, I assumed inside of her. The animalistic nature of it all somehow broke the spell I was under. Embarrassed, I quickly slammed the door shut and literally ran back to my office.*

That was about three years ago, and I've never looked at Tony St. Clair the same. I *still* can't look him in the eye.

His deep baritone beckoned for me to enter. When I did, I headed directly to the executive black leather chair sitting in front of his desk. He glanced over his shoulder as I settled and finished tapping out a reply on his cell phone. Putting it back into the pocket of his slacks, he began pouring a drink at his bar.

I took the time to appreciate what a beautiful man he truly was. About six four, two hundred thirty pounds, not fat, but certainly a sizable man. Toned muscles from what I can remember when I saw him naked that day and wide shoulders. Can I talk about his skin? Made me wonder about his skin regimen. Smooth—no man should have skin that smooth. The color, pecan brown, with a nicely trimmed full beard and mustache. Not to mention the bald head. Never had I been a fan of bald men before, but I must admit Tony St. Clair made it look good. If he wasn't such an asshole, I would find him irresistible. The total package. Every woman's fantasy. But there was something to be said for a nice, positive attitude.

"Miss McMillan, did you hear what I said?" he bellowed, bringing me out of my daydream. I was grateful for the melanin in my skin because it meant he couldn't see the tinge of red waft over my face in embarrassment.

My shoulders slumped at being caught unfocused on the job at hand. "I'm sorry, Mr. St. Clair, my mind drifted. What did you say?"

"I said, is that my coffee?"

"Oh, yes, sir. I'm sorry." I placed the lukewarm coffee on his desk and opened my planner to begin reminding him about his meetings. He liked to know his daily plans first thing in the morning, even though I linked his calendar with mine, so he had access. It was extremely annoying to me, but it was what he liked, and he was the boss. "You're supposed to meet with the board of trustees at nine a.m. and then a conference call with Wright Tech at ten thirty," I rattled off.

I glanced up, noticing him watching me, and wondered

briefly if there was something on my face. Subconsciously, I wiped my hand down my face, hoping whatever he saw was no longer there. Mentally, I went over my morning routine. Did I forget to wash my face? That couldn't be it. I applied light makeup before I left home, which was why I was late. Mr. St. Clair staring at me like I was an object was beginning to make me uncomfortable.

"Is something wrong, sir?" I finally asked, trying to keep the concern from my voice. What exactly was the problem? It wasn't the coffee. He hadn't touched it yet.

"Nothing, continue, please." He leaned back in his chair, waiting for me to announce what's next.

With three meetings confirmed, I closed my planner and rose from my seat. As I turned and headed for the door, he stopped me in my tracks.

"Remi. Sit. We're not finished." He never called me by my first name, even though I insisted for the past three years. Never once had he broken protocol. *Oh hell,* I thought as I slowly made the death walk back to my seat. I spied the coffee I bought in his hand.

I plopped down in the seat immediately, trying to defend myself. "Mr. St. Clair, I'm so sorry the coffee is cold. I didn't realize how late I was until I got to the elevator," I rushed.

He raised a hand to stop my rambling and placed the cup back down on the desk. "Maybe next time, don't be late. I would hate to fire you." He pierced my soul with those soft caramel-colored eyes.

My heart was beating so fast that I just nodded, not sure whether or not my voice would crack if I answered him. Why did this man wreck my nerves? He wasn't a terrible boss, but he terrified me, and I really didn't like it.

"I need you to reserve rooms for my meeting with Transient Technologies in Chicago next month." The *click, click* of the mouse echoed through the room as I waited for his instructions.

"Yes, sir. How many rooms?" I gave a curt nod while opening my planner to the notes section.

During the three years I'd worked for Mr. St. Clair, I'd learned to write the important things down. Which meant pretty much everything he said during our morning meetings. I crossed my legs, ready to take notes. I'd learned my lesson the hard way, without going into too much detail, let's just say it was a complete mess! And something I hadn't repeated.

"Two adjacent rooms, on the top floor with balconies overlooking the Chicago River. The penthouses, in case it wasn't obvious," he reiterated. I jotted down his specifications, silently repeating the list to make sure I'd got it right.

Mr. St. Clair liked his luxuries and his comforts. The rooms needed to include private gyms, luxury bathrooms, and Jacuzzis. I added those amenities to the list as well. I think he liked the privacy of it all. He was a man always in the spotlight. When he went out into the world, the media followed him incessantly, so he needed that time to himself.

"How many days, sir?" He was silent for a moment, and it caused me to once again glance up from my work. Like before, he was watching me, and it was unnerving to say the least. "Sir? Is something wrong?"

I couldn't help but ask again while fidgeting in my seat under his scrutiny. Despite the three years I had worked for him, he still made me jittery. I mean the guy was a behemoth, but he never made me uncomfortable.

Until today.

Readjusting myself in my seat, I uncrossed and crossed my legs, making a mental note to be conscientious when around him as his eyes followed my movements. Filled with lust, his gingerbread-colored orbs cut back to mine. There had to be a mistake. I was sure my eyes were just playing tricks on me.

"A week, for now, then I'll play it by ear. I have no clue how long the negotiations will take," he spoke, rising from the dark wood desk. He glanced once again at his watch, which made me turn to the clock hanging on the wall to the right of me. It was almost time for his meeting. "That will be all."

Grateful to be dismissed, I was certainly glad that was over. I scurried to the door as if my ass was on fire back to my office. I settled behind my desk, but try as I might, I couldn't concentrate, wondering what the fuck just happened.

CHAPTER TWO

"Fuck," I mumbled under my breath as I watched my personal assistant hightail it out of my office after she caught me ogling her. She was alarmed, which was the last thing I wanted. She was nervous enough around me, but I needed her to stay with the company for several reasons. One, she was the best goddamn assistant I ever had. Efficient, hardworking, and *usually* on time. And two, Remi was gorgeous as hell, and she didn't even recognize how lovely she really was. I must admit that her beauty was one of the reasons I hired her. Might make me an ass, but I loved beautiful women.

Remi was about five seven, two hundred pounds, and thick in all the right places. Big full breasts, hips, ass, and long, long legs. Many nights I jacked off just thinking about what that body looked like without all those frumpy clothes she wore. I suspected she tried to hide herself, but I could *see.*

Ever since she caught me fucking Leah in my office, I noticed she could hardly look me in the eye anymore. I gotta admit that fact bothered me, which was the main reason I was a total dick to her. I mean, making her buy me a coffee every morning that I don't even drink had to be at the top of the dick list. I shook her, and in a way…some sick, perverted way, I enjoyed the reaction I got from her. What grinds my gears was the fact that she *did* get under my skin.

It all started about three months ago. I was out with Ashley, an old friend I grew up with. There was never anything sexual between us, we just liked to have fun sometimes. She kept me grounded and was my connection to not forgetting where I came from. We did normal things, like going to the movies or out to eat at fast-food restaurants. This particular night, we left the movies and went for a drink at the bar down from the theater. It was perfect. Not too packed, nor hot and uncomfortable, a live band, and the sounds of people laughing and talking. As soon as we walked in, I noticed Remi on the dance floor. I couldn't take my eyes off her hypnotic aura. She was laughing, carefree…and sexy as hell. She tipped the bottle in her hand upward to kiss those luscious lips, and a zing of lust went straight to my dick. The thought of what those lips would feel like wrapped around my length stopped me short. Never had I thought anything sexual about her before, even when she watched me fuck Leah, not once. Sure, she was beautiful, but I never saw *her.* Not like that night.

"Who is she?" Ashley asked. I had to practically rip my gaze away from Remi but sat where I could still see her.

"What makes you think I know?" I quipped, irritated Ashley caught me staring at Remi.

Ashley reached for the drink menu having already decided, apparently while I was in my daydream, what she was going to eat. I grabbed the food menu and flipped through it.

"Well, you haven't stopped looking at her since we came through the door," she smirked, continuing to browse the menu.

I cleared my throat, realizing she was right. "She's my personal assistant, but I've never"—I waved my hand in Remi's direction on the makeshift dance floor—"seen her like this."

"Ahhh." She clicked her tongue, signaling for a waitress.

We ordered our drinks and food. "What's that supposed to mean?" Frustration rose in my chest as my eyes wandered back to Remi on the dance floor. She was sensual…graceful. Beautiful.

"Nothing," she denied, as she turned to watch Remi over her shoulder. "Gorgeous, isn't she?" Ashley wasn't into women, but she was always honest when it came to complimenting another woman on her beauty.

"I guess." I tried to play it off.

As soon as my beer arrived, I took a deep, long swig, relieved I had something to distract me from the conversation and Remi's dancing. Soon after our food arrived, Ashley understood my silence and dropped the discussion. I appreciated it, but for some reason, that silence didn't stop my eyes from tracking Remi. When she moved to the bar for another drink, my eyes followed her. I got inexplicably irritated when the guy she was dancing with put his hands on her round hips. I wanted to punch him in the face for touching what should be mine. Seeing her brush him away had me breathe an inward sigh of relief. When she moved from the bar toward the restroom with her girlfriend, I couldn't keep my eyes from the hallway, waiting for her to return.

This behavior was unusual, and it didn't sit well with me. In all the time I'd been watching her, she hadn't noticed me, and for some reason I was strangely pleased. I didn't think she would want to run into me outside of work because we didn't have that type of relationship.

That night when I arrived at my house, I didn't bother turning on any lights. I rushed up the stairs, taking them two at a time, and hit the shower. By the time I stripped out of my clothes, I was hard and ready to release. Turning on the shower, I tested the water's temperature before I stepped in and allowed the cascade to cover me from head to toe. I closed my eyes and conjured up my new favorite fantasy, *Remi*. In my mind, she looked exactly how she did tonight. Not the stuffy, all-business, no-play personal assistant I saw five days a week. The way she moved, and her smiling face were fixed in my mind's eye as I palmed my dick. I tugged my stiffness to the beat of her swaying hips as I envisioned my hands around her waist. Our bodies moved together in tantric rhapsody on the dance floor in tune to the beat.

I focused on the steady rhythm of the water beating down on my body, on the moves rhythmically executed by her thick frame. The sensations overwhelmed me, and before I knew it, I came… HARD. After catching my breath, I finished my shower and went to bed. I couldn't process what this was. I didn't know if it was euphoria from the hardest orgasm I'd ever experienced in my life or if it was the drinks I had at the bar with Ashley. Either way, I needed to sleep on whatever was happening. Time shifted slowly before I drifted off to sleep, with Remi still on my mind. Now what the fuck am I supposed to do?

My morning meeting was a blur. My mind was so full of Remi that my thoughts were all over the place. What the hell the trustees decided, I had no clue. Hell, I didn't even stay the whole meeting. In the middle of the budget presentation, I just left. I'd never done anything like that before. You don't get to be one of the most successful businessmen in the world doing things like walking out of meetings about money. I asked the board to inform me of their decision, and I would help in any way I could.

I needed to get my shit together. My next move was the negotiations with Wright Tech, a company I wanted to absorb into St. Clair Technologies. The company was innovative but hadn't generated the funds needed to keep up with the production of its software and marketing of the company. I had a few minutes before the call, so I took some time to relax. Closing my eyes, I leaned back in my chair and tried to get a handle on the situation. For the first time since Remi left my office, I was able to get centered.

In the middle of trying to clear my head of Remi, my phone rang. Glancing at my watch, I realized it was time for the one o'clock conference call. Grabbing the receiver, I recited my name at the automated prompt and pressed one to join the call.

"Hello? St. Clair, are you there?" Mr. Wright, the company founder, questioned him coolly.

"I'm here, Martin. How have you been?"

"Good. Will be even better once we get down to the business at hand," he spoke confidently.

That was fine by me, I hated small talk. I preferred to get right down to business, but I didn't make my millions by making the people I did business with feel inferior. I could be a bulldog when it came to getting what I wanted, but Martin was eager for this transaction because of the amount of money on the table. I met Martin Wright once. We ran into each other at a conference and hit it off for the most part. Back then, he was just starting out and had an infectious exuberance about him. We exchanged information, although at the time I was sure I wasn't going to call him or set up any meetings. But I kept an eye on him and his company. When rumors started circulating the company was in trouble, I reached out, and thankfully, Martin answered. He was a savvy businessman, and with adequate backing, his company wouldn't fail. And so here we are.

"Have your lawyers looked over the contract yet?" I scribbled a few notes on the pad in front of me, eager to get the deal done.

"They have, and according to Riley everything looks fair." There was a pause followed by a sigh coming from his end.

"What's the sigh for then?"

"I just want to thank you for stepping in. I'm a little in over my head with this company," Martin admitted.

I thought about what I should say to this young man. At twenty-five, Martin Wright started a tech company on his own that had caught *my* eye. That was an achievement in itself. If nothing else, he had impeccable tenacity and would go far.

"Martin, I'm about to pay you a lot of money for your company. If you want, just start from scratch with something new. You'll have the capital to pour into it once this deal goes through."

He hadn't even thought about the money he would get, let alone what to do with it. I could tell his spirits were a little higher than they were before. His excitement became apparent over the line, and it made me smile. "Damn, you're right. Let's get this done."

I remembered a time when my potential work excited me. "I'll have my lawyer contact Riley, and we'll get the paperwork done to make this thing official," I reassured him that the deal was pretty much done. Out of everything I handled daily, acquiring one of the best up-and-coming companies to add to my empire had to be the icing on the proverbial cake.

By the time we ended the call, it was already lunchtime. Normally I would go out for lunch, but today for some reason I decided to stay close to the office. On the way to the elevator, I approached Remi's office and noticed her door was open.

Maybe she'll like to have lunch with me, I speculated. Peeking inside her empty office, a part of me wondered where she'd gone without saying a word. "Of course, she did, idiot. It's lunchtime," I mumbled aloud.

I never kept tabs on my employees' lunch schedules because as corporate employees, it was a part of our work culture to maintain a certain level of trust from us both, and I trusted them to be reasonable. Stepping off the elevator onto the third floor, I turned right and headed into the cafeteria. Mouthwatering smells, wafting throughout the surrounding space, had my stomach growling in a matter of seconds. I scanned the area, trying to decide exactly what it was I wanted. With no taste for anything particular, I wandered to the grill loaded with steaks, burgers, and hot dogs on one end. On the other end was a hibachi grill. The chef grilled onions, zucchini, shredded carrots, chopped steak, and mushrooms in front of his hungry customers, plating the vegetables and steak on top of a bowl of rice. With my decision made, I stepped in line behind two ladies who worked in accounting.

One of the women turned to me with a warm smile stretched across her face. "How are you, Mr. St. Clair?" she cheesed, grabbing her plate from the chef.

I returned her greeting with the same smile, coupled with a head nod. "I'm fine, thank you." The women looked at one another, giggling as they moved off to sit at their table of waiting friends.

While ordering, I was acutely aware of the whispers, side-eyed glances, and pointed fingers when my head was turned. I caught snippets of, "I can't believe he is eating in here." And "Hmph, looks like someone finally came down from his throne." I worked hard for that throne. Deserved to sit on it. I ignored the commentary and concentrated on my food being prepared. When the chef finished, I accepted my plate and grabbed a bottle of water, deciding to go back to my office and eat because I preferred to eat in peace. Despite my position, I didn't care to be the center of attention right now.

Just then, a laugh I remembered from my dreams filled the room. I scanned the cafeteria a second time to find her at a table near the outer wall. Remi was sitting with two other women next to a floor-to-ceiling window looking out over the city. She wasn't aware of me, and I wanted to keep it that way. I wanted to watch her in her comfort zone. Yeah, it might sound a bit stalkerish, but if she knew I was in the vicinity, I was almost certain she would shut down.

Focused on observing her in her element, I was so enamored with her that I hadn't noticed the lunch hour ending so quickly. The din surrounding us quickly faded, and I was now a part of the scene instead of sticking out like a sore thumb. For the better part of forty minutes, I watched Remi laugh with and tease her friends. I had to admit, I liked this Remi. She was captivating, like that night we saw her at the bar. When I finished my lunch, I decided to walk over and say hi. Leaving my plate on the table, I stood up, adjusted my suit jacket, and sauntered over to where she sat. Her back was to me as I approached, however, her two lunch partners sat silently with their mouths gaped open.

I cleared my throat before speaking, "Miss McMillan."

The tension in her shoulders was evident as she turned slowly to face me. "Mr. St. Clair." There was a hint of worry in her voice as those deep brown eyes slid toward the clock on the wall facing the room. Realizing she was checking to see if she was late, I took advantage of the opportunity to show her a softer side of me when she began to rise slowly from her seat.

"No need to get up. Come to my office when you're finished. I forgot to mention a few details in our meeting this morning." I hoped that knowing there was no rush for her to leave would help her relax a little around me.

"Yes, sir. I'll be there soon," she said, looking over her shoulder at me.

Her deep russet eyes stretched wide, still in shock like everyone else, I paid a visit to the cafeteria. I nodded and walked out, heading back to my office. As I reached the elevator, I realized I was fucked. For the first time ever in my adult life, I had no clue what I would do with a striking, yet forbidden, woman just within my reach.

CHAPTER THREE

I gawked as my boss walked away from my table, *not* being a complete ass for once. His suit jacket pulled taut as he buttoned the two buttons on the jacket, showing off those broad, toned shoulders.

"Yummy," Erica proclaimed, pulling me out of my head and away from the retreating broad back of Mr. St. Clair.

I turned to face her. "What?"

I looked at all our empty plates, and no one was having dessert. Confusion laced my features as I shrugged my shoulders, not understanding what was delicious.

"Mr. St. Clair's yummy," she stated, as if it was a fact.

What am I saying? It *was* facts! The man was too fine for his own good. Too bad he had such an awful attitude.

"I guess," I shrugged my shoulders nonchalantly. There was no way I would admit I agreed with her. As a matter of fact, no one would ever hear me say anything of that nature about him. Not even Erica.

Erica and I started at St. Clair Technologies around the same time, but we've known one another a lot longer. She was the first person I befriended when I came to New York. I met Erica at the same coffee shop two blocks down from the St. Clair building where I got my coffee every morning. She was sitting at the only booth not filled with people. She let me join her when we caught eyes while I was searching for a seat. We hit it off as soon as I sat down. And now, years later, we still meet at that coffee shop at least three times a week to catch up.

Erica was my best friend. She was wild, carefree, and I lived vicariously through her more often than not. She loved to go to clubs and bars where she could drink and dance all night. She went on blind dates with the guys she met on Tinder, and I cringed with fear every time she came back to tell me about one of her dates. She was the total opposite of me, although I did have fun occasionally. More than once, I'd gotten a late-night or early morning phone call to come pick her up from some place or another. I'd give her a talking to. She'd listen to my tirade and then go back to living it up. But she always knew I was there for her. Like loyal friends should be, we were there for one another. I'd never been let down once.

Erica also had a healthy sex life, which unfortunately, she didn't spare me the details of. So, her summation of our boss was not a surprise to me. She often tried to get me to double date with her or even set me up on blind dates, but I had no interest. I was not hard-pressed for sex and was content to use my vibrator when frustrated. My heart had been broken more than once, and I was not in a hurry to have it broken again. I turned down double dates, preferring to go out alone or with her and a few other friends.

I smiled and shrugged my shoulders at Erica when she reacted with a look of shock at my indifference to our boss. "Look, he's a dick. No matter how fine he might be, attitude says a *whole* lot more about a person than what they look like," I proclaimed. Gathering my things, I glanced at the clock once more and realized if I didn't leave, I *would* be late from lunch. "I'll call you," I yelled over my shoulder as I scurried to the elevator.

It was then I realized Mr. St. Clair didn't grill me this morning about being late. As a matter of fact, he seemed less like his usual self. He was borderline…*nice.* I wondered what the catch was, and you could believe I would be waiting for the other shoe to drop. When I reached my office, I grabbed my planner and ink pen, then sped toward his door. I knocked again, like always since that fateful first day, and waited for permission to enter.

"Remi come in." I opened the door and stepped through, closing it firmly behind me. "Have a seat," he commanded.

Saying my first name again. What's the deal?

I took my seat like he suggested.

"What do you need?" I inquired, pulling out my pen and turning to the page I scribbled my notes on from our morning meeting.

"I forgot to mention it this morning, but can you get in contact with my flight crew for the trip to Chicago? I've decided to fly private instead of commercial." I gave a curt nod as I jotted his new instructions into my notes. "And can you include a chef and a full bar at my disposal?"

I wrote everything down, adding it to my already extensive list. "I put the flight crew on my list this morning, sir, assuming you'd want some privacy to unwind before the meetings," I rushed, hoping I hadn't overstepped my boundaries.

He seemed pleased with my assumption, and for some reason his pleasure made me warm inside. Pride swelled through me, but I shook it off. Buried the sensation deep down inside and read over my list just to break eye contact and regain my composure.

"Is there anything else, Mr. St. Clair?"

There were a lot of things I needed to take care of for this trip. For most of the morning, I'd been doing paperwork, setting up his appointments, and confirming meetings. I had yet to get the rooms for Chicago, and I needed to take care of that before I did anything else.

I looked down at my list, prioritizing what to work on first, when I noticed he hadn't answered my question. Tearing myself away from the page, our eyes locked. He was gawking *again.* "Is there anything else, sir?" I asked more forcefully than I'd liked, breaking the awkwardness.

"No. Nothing else, Miss McMillan. You may go."

He dismissed me, and I was all too grateful to retreat to my office. After closing my door, I took a deep breath. I didn't know why he was off-putting. The relief I felt at being back in the confines of my office rapidly reduced my heart rate. Soon I was able to take in a breath without the wobbliness of overactive nerves. Since I caught him watching me this morning, I didn't know what to do or how to act in his presence. I rocked my head back and forth to clear it from the revelation and got back to work. I turned on my computer and began my hotel search, which yielded several prospects.

The first two hotels were booked solid. I could have dropped his name to get them to cancel someone's reservation but decided against it because that would be wrong of me. I came to the last hotel on the list. "Please let this one be it," I prayed to no one in particular. It wasn't often I failed at a task Mr. St. Clair gave me, and I wasn't about to start any of that nonsense now. Once I gave his name, the clerk gasped, a typical reaction. She was more than eager to help with anything I needed.

"I have two rooms for Mr. St. Clair, ma'am. Is there anything else we can help you with?"

"No thank you. All I need is the confirmation number so I can relay it to Mr. St. Clair."

"Sure." She rattled off the sixteen-digit number, and I wrote it in my planner.

"Can you also email it to me?"

"Of course," she agreed. I gave her my email address, listening to the echo of the keys of her computer as she typed.

"Yes, ma'am. You should get the email any moment now," she reassured. "Thank you so much for doing business with us. You have a great rest of the day."

"Thank you. You too," I replied and hung up. After signing into my email, I confirmed and forwarded the confirmation number to Mr. St. Clair. "On to the next one," I mused aloud.

I enjoyed the days when I was busy because it made the time go by more quickly. Today was productive but also different. Different because Mr. St. Clair had not once made me go get him a midday coffee. Usually, like clockwork, no matter what I was doing, I dropped everything and went to the coffee shop. The one time I thought he had a routine, and I went for his coffee, he jumped down my throat. Said he didn't want the coffee and dropped it in the trash. I was appalled at his rudeness, but from then on, I waited for his call. He hadn't been his normal ornery self today. And without the interruptions, I'd gotten plenty of work done.

I perused my planner for the next meeting and buzzed his office to remind him. "Mr. St. Clair." I paused for his acknowledgment.

"Yes," came his deep baritone through the receiver.

God, if I didn't know what kind of man he really was, his voice would melt me into a puddle.

"You have a four o'clock in fifteen minutes."

"Thank you, Miss McMillan. I'm going home afterward," he informed me before he hung up.

"Not one for chitchat," I muttered, hanging up my phone.

My last task of the day consisted of me lining up a chef. What he needed with a chef for a flight that was a little over two hours, who knew? With his love for seafood, I focused my search on a chef who could do fantastic and amazing dishes with fish, as well as everyday comfort foods. By five in the evening, I'd called at least five chefs. Fortunately, the last one on the list was on leave from his restaurant and was available for the right price.

One thing I could say was money was no object when it came to the employees of Tony St. Clair. I was lucky to have landed this job. I was out of work when I came to New York. Although I do a lot for Mr. St. Clair, he paid me my worth, as well as everyone else who worked in this building.

A knock on my office door stopped me from gathering my things to head home. Erica meandered into my office ready to make our after-work doughnut and coffee run. One could never have too much coffee.

"What's up? You ready?" She scooped my bag from the chair in front of me and held an arm out as I came around my desk.

"Yes, I'm ready," I mused, slinging my bag over my shoulder. "I can't wait. It's been a busy day." After locking my door, we headed toward the elevator. "You didn't have to come up here. You could've waited for me in the lobby." I smirked, knowing full well she hoped to catch a glimpse of the boss.

I grinned when she craned her neck toward the double doors, confirming my suspicions. It was one of the many things I envied about Erica. If she saw something she wanted, she went for it with no apologies or regrets. I wanted to be able to say that I didn't regret any of my decisions, especially the dumb ones.

I wasn't a New York native. I was from a small town in North Carolina with a population of around two hundred thousand. I ended up here after running from one of my stupid decisions named Mark. I thought he loved me, but…WRONG! Turned out he loved three women, including me. Humiliated, I simply packed my things, threw them in my car, told my father I loved him, and left for New York without even telling him what happened. My situation with Mark left me untrusting of men, I hadn't had sex or, for that matter, been in a meaningful relationship in at least a year. That's a long time for a healthy black woman in her mid-thirties to go without intimacy.

All the way to the shop I debated telling Erica about the weirdness of the day because she'd take it and run with it, coming up with all types of scenarios where the boss and I would live happily ever after. I rolled my eyes at the thought but believed she wouldn't break my trust and blabber it all over the building. By the time we reached the shop, ordered our coffee and doughnuts, then found a booth in the back, I decided I'd tell my friend.

While Erica recapped her weekend, I just blurted it out before I lost my nerve. "I think Mr. St. Clair has a crush on me."

I mean, I sounded like I was still in high school or something, but I couldn't describe it any other way. I took a big swig of my white chocolate mocha before I said anything else. Erica's attention was on me, and her mouth hung open in disbelief. "Wait, what? When?"

I ran down for her what happened in his office that morning. "I caught him ogling my legs this morning at our meeting. He likes a rundown of everything he has lined up for the day," I explained. "He got all silent and didn't answer when I questioned him for clarity." I took a bite of my doughnut, trying to gather my thoughts.

"Oh my gosh," she exclaimed. "I knew it! Damn it, I knew it!!"

I scanned the room, making sure no one was listening to her outburst. Erica was giddy about gossip. "SHHHHH!" Once she quieted down, I began again. "Erica, I swear, when our eyes locked, there was something," I whispered almost inaudibly. I didn't want anyone knowing about *any* of this. Many of the people who worked at St. Clair Technologies frequented this place.

"Something like what?"

She had barely touched her doughnut and coffee as she

became ensnared by my story. It was not often that I was the one with the juicy gossip to spill. I thought for a moment.

Maybe I was wrong and just saw what I wanted to in his eyes. No, I know what I saw.

"Lust? Want? I don't know," I told her as my shoulders suddenly felt burdened. This whole thing was overwhelming to me. I had to massage my temple to release some stress.

"Wow," she sighed.

"Yeah wow. Every time I get near him, I'm fidgety and on edge. I've never been like that around a man. I mean granted I don't have as much experience as you," I snickered.

She gasped, "Bitch, what's that supposed to mean?" We both laughed out loud because she knew I was right. Erica's easy visage turned to concern. "He hasn't tried anything, has he? I mean, why are you so jumpy? You need me to kick his ass?"

I looked up over the rim of my cup and saw she was serious about her threat. But at the same time, why am I anxious around Mr. St. Clair?

I shook my head furiously. "Don't you dare. He's never been anything but respectful and professional toward me. Him being short, blunt, and an asshole, doesn't count. He has been okay today. Besides, your hits would probably feel like a baby's fists against him," I tittered.

We both sat back in our seats and finished our doughnuts and coffee in silence. I imagined her trying to come up with a reason, just like I was, why, all of a sudden, our boss would set his sights on me. This entire thing might be my imagination, though. We headed out the door and promised to meet in the morning. Erica continued down the street, walking two blocks in the opposite direction to her apartment, and I waited for the *Lyft* I ordered before we departed.

I lived in New Rochelle, about thirty minutes from Manhattan, but with traffic it was a little longer than that. New Rochelle was voted number 18 on the list of "Most Diverse Cities in

America," according to *Wallet Hub* (whatever that was). But I could see why it boasted of the diversity. It was present in the building where I live.

The complex consisted of six apartments. There was me, the only African American woman in the building, an Asian guy named Charlie Park—everyone called him Park—who was never home. Also, in his thirties like me. Rashida was from the Middle East—I forget where, though. Ronnie is a white guy from Texas. Alexia Trejo moved here from the Bronx—she reminded me of J-Lo in the movie, *Gigli,* with Ben Affleck. Her parents were originally from Puerto Rico, but moved to New York just before she was born, and then there's Mack, also African American. He was a former football player until he busted his knee and was now a bouncer at one of the bars here. I liked my neighbors. We all get along because we have different lifestyles. We're not inconveniencing one another when we're home. Sometimes we got together to have a cookout or gathered at an apartment to drink, listen to music, or watch a game.

New Rochelle was building and expanding, and I had to say I loved it. The city outside the city. It was what drew me here in the first place. My apartment wasn't a dump, but like most things in New York, it could use some renovation to keep up with the changing times. To enter the building, a keycard was required for the gate and the main building. It was one of the reasons I chose this place. I felt safe here, and the neighborhood was friendly. Though it wasn't a penthouse, I did, however, have creature comforts. Since I had been working at St. Clair Technologies, I was able to upgrade from thrift store furniture to new, modern sets. There weren't any children in the building. Most of the tenants are single, young to middle-aged people like me. All except Mack, I believe. He was a little older than the rest of us.

I lived on the top floor and rarely used the elevator, preferring to use the stairs to keep in shape. But today was an elevator day because I still couldn't wrap my head around the actions of my boss toward me. I hoped I wasn't reading too much into it.

By the time I entered my apartment, I had all but resigned myself to forget that anything happened. I glanced at the clock on the wall, and it was already seven o'clock. I had just enough time to take a shower and have a microwave dinner before I settled down with an enjoyable book.

CHAPTER FOUR

Another fucking sleepless night. It was two in the morning, and if I didn't get some sleep soon, there would be hell to pay. But I couldn't get Remi out of my head. I didn't know what the hell I was going to do. I was so hard, it was uncomfortable, and I kept seeing her body every time I closed my eyes. Those legs were a secret pathway leading to her treasure.

I palmed my dick and released a guttural groan. That shit felt so good. At thirty-eight with plenty of money, I had my share of women, many of them attracted by my riches. I knew it from the jump and treated them accordingly. But no one had ever been more off limits and frustrating than Remi. I jacked off every night to images of her, since no one had been in my bed since I saw Remi shake her luscious ass at that bar all those months ago. She was the only one I wanted, but I couldn't have her. It was a struggle to say the least.

I tried to relax. Closing my eyes, I easily pictured her. I've watched her so many times without her knowing, conjuring her image came easily. It was a bit creepy, but I couldn't break the hold she had on me. The infatuation I had for her was going to cause me to go insane if she wasn't mine soon. I pulled at my dick, causing it to harden and lengthen in my hand as I imagined myself taking her from behind over my desk as her cries and moans made my senses more heightened. I jerked harder until the tell-tell tingle came over my body, and my balls tightened up. I never called a woman's name during sex in my life, but as I came, Remi's name was on my lips. I panted hard, as if I were hyperventilating. I drew in several deep breaths, to normalize my breathing, before heading to the bathroom to clean myself. My body was sated and exhausted. When I made my way back to bed, I relaxed under the covers and drifted off to a dreamless sleep.

ONE MONTH LATER

I'd been obsessing over Remi for the last few months. The complete infatuation was not going away. I'd made up in my mind I wanted her in my bed. *Soon.* My plan was simple. She was coming with me to Chicago. However, I decided not to tell her until the very last possible moment. That way, she wouldn't have a chance to say no or back out at the last second. The kicker was making the change to the reservation she made over a month ago, canceling the second room. It was the only way I could ensure I would have the opportunity to reel her in. When we arrived at the hotel, there would only be one room, one bed. The second part of my plan was to release my charms on her. There wasn't a woman alive who could resist me. Remi would be the first woman I actually pursued for a long term, happily ever after relationship. She'd have no choice but to let me in. It would work. I was positive it would work. It *must* work because my desperation for Remi had taken over.

I thought about the plan long and hard for the past few

weeks. "It would work because she won't be able to say no," I reasoned aloud with myself. *And if she asked why?* "If she asks, I'll just tell her I need the meetings transcribed by someone I can trust." It wasn't a secret in the business world that the owner of Transient Technologies, Steven Smith, was dirty.

These last few weeks leading up to this trip, I made sure not to slip up watching her again. Oh, I still fantasized about caressing her body while we were together, but I never let her see my desire. A mistake I hadn't made again since that day at the office. I admit, though, it wasn't easy. But in the meantime, I managed to make her hate me even more than she already did by being a complete asshole to her. To be honest, it was a part of the annoyance I harbored inside for her. If she was a minute late, I laid into her. If my coffee was lukewarm, I ripped her. And every single time I did, my heart tore in two. Guilt and shame racked my consciousness.

She was distancing herself from me, our morning meetings had become brief and tense. She braced herself when I spoke to her. She answered the phone with a tremble in her voice. She walked on eggshells around me. I made her twitchy, even more than before, but now I wondered if, somehow, I'd broken her spirit. God, I hated myself. I felt like the worst human being on the planet. Which was why, with this trip to Chicago, I'd make up for everything I'd done to her these past few months.

I glanced at my watch.

Lunchtime.

I decided to stop by Remi's office and ask her to lunch. Hopefully, she'd see I wasn't the devil I'd been showing her lately. Her door was open, but her office was empty. There was only one place she could be. I made a beeline for the elevator and headed to the third-floor cafeteria.

As soon as I stepped into the room, my eyes automatically scanned for her, finally spotting her sitting at the same table with the same group of women as before. Her plate was empty, and they were conversing. It would be a waste of my time to ask.

I resigned myself to watching her from afar like always. For the past month, I ate my lunch here in this room because, more than likely, I'd get to watch Remi in her natural element. Her interaction with others was fluid. She didn't seem agitated, and she kept a smile on her face. All differing responses from when she was with me. The plus side was that I wasn't the enigma my employees thought I was. They were getting used to me being here, so there were no whispers like before. I could sit and enjoy lunch.

I took a seat a few tables away from Remi and her friends. Her laughter rang out from the other side of the room and caressed my spirit. It was the sweetest sound I'd heard that day. Steak forgotten, my eyes were drawn to her. When she let her guard down, she was so stunning and most beautiful to me.

Her cinnamon skin was even and smooth in the natural light from the windows, and her hair shined as if she had a halo around her head when the sun hit just right. The moment reminded me of when I saw her dancing at the bar, and I discreetly adjusted myself under the table. I couldn't approach her with a hard-on, that would definitely be a problem. I made quick work of my savory steak. Closing my eyes, I willed my dick to calm down. I had to think of something else, or I was never gonna be able to get up from this table. I thought about the most reprehensible thing I could, a video I recently saw on *Twitter* of a young man playing basketball. He went up for a block and came back down with a broken finger. The bone protruded out of the skin perpendicular to the rest of his hand as the blood continuously dripped from his finger. I shivered, as I could literally feel his pain.

"Okay, that did the trick," I muttered to myself.

I finished my water and rose from my seat, heading over to

Remi's table. As I approached, one woman leaned into Remi and gestured her head toward me, trying to get Remi's attention.

I cleared my throat. "Afternoon, ladies."

In unison, they replied, "Good afternoon, Mr. St. Clair." Except Remi. She sat with her back ramrod straight and stiff. She didn't even turn my way.

"Good afternoon, Miss McMillan." She slowly turned in my direction. Her eyes caressed my enormous frame until she reached my orbs. The sudden thrill shooting through my body was unexpected, but I relished the sensation. She wanted me just as much as I wanted her.

"Mr. St. Clair, may I help you?" I didn't blame her for the coldness in her tone. I understood her initial emotions toward me and took it as an excellent sign that she craved me.

"Yes. I would like to see you in my office as soon as you return. There are some changes to tomorrow's trip." I spoke curtly, nodding my goodbyes to her as well as her friends. She would be at my office immediately afterward. Remi was the type of professional who didn't like last-minute changes to plans supposedly set in stone. My plan was going to be successful. I had a good feeling about what I set in motion. Smiling to myself, *now I only needed to cancel that second room.*

CHAPTER FIVE

I knew he was there before he even cleared his throat to address us. I'd smelled that same cologne for the past three years. It was heady and had me dizzy with lust every time I got a whiff of it. Mr. St. Clair had a hold on my senses, and I didn't quite know what to do about it. I was in euphoria with him standing near me, and when I turned in his direction, after he addressed me, my eyes and desire overrode my good common sense and caressed every inch of his body until they locked with his. I hoped he didn't see the longing there or the want I had for him. After the past few weeks, I didn't even know why I was intensely crushing on him. He was awful to me and had me off-balance. I was afraid to do my job for fear of his reaction.

Mr. St. Clair had turned me into mush, and I was beginning to resent him for it. Because of that fact, I should be irritated with myself for even wanting him. To my relief there was no indication he took heed of my shamelessness. In fact, he hadn't once looked at me inappropriately since that day almost a month ago in his office when I caught him ogling my legs. I discussed it with Erica, and we both concluded I had been wrong about what

I saw. I brought my attention back to my boss, greeting him properly, realizing I was borderline rude. He wanted to meet with me in his office after lunch to discuss changes to his trip to Chicago tomorrow. I worked extra hard not to roll my eyes because I hated last-minute plans. Especially changes to the plans I spent hours arranging. So as soon as he made his way out of the cafeteria, I gathered my things and followed him.

A moment later, my heels echoed across the floor, heading to the small hallway where my office was located. I plucked my planner and pen off my desk, then headed to the double doors at the end of the hall. Like always, I knocked lightly and waited for permission to enter.

"Come in," his melodic voice wafted out to me. His voice ensnared me as I closed my eyes for a few seconds to take it in. I stepped into the room and closed the door behind me. "Thank you again. We'll be seeing you soon," he said and ended his call.

I took my seat across from him, flipped my planner open, and waited.

"Thank you for coming so soon, but you didn't need to cut your lunch short." His lips turned up into a smile that dazzled me. I imagined that smile also melted panties whenever he flashed it at a female.

He was being nice. Why was he being so nice? For the better part of a month, this man had been on my neck and ass about every little slip-up, so what was the deal?

"You're welcome. It's nothing, really. We were finished anyway. Only talking," I rambled. "You wanted to make changes to your plans?"

"Ahhh, yes. You need to come with me to Chicago tomorrow." *Wait? What?* There was no lead-up, no warning, just I'm going. I'd never gone with him before. Why did I have to go this time?

"Excuse me?" My mind was in overdrive. I didn't believe it, I needed clarification. I didn't have time to prepare or anything.

"Did you say I have to go to Chicago? But sir, I'm not prepared," I sputtered, my mind reeling as I thought about all the tasks I needed to get done before tomorrow. "Why do you need me to go?" I panicked. A list of things to do formulated in my mind. I had to pack on top of double-checking the arrangements I'd made for his trip. I had already checked the room bookings, those were fine. Mr. St. Clair must've been able to see I was freaking out. I heard him say my name.

"Remi," he called quietly. Noticing I was still on edge and hadn't responded, "Miss McMillan." His booming voice startled me to attention. I met his eyes, and they softened as he gazed at me. "Calm down. You don't need to worry about anything. I'll take care of it. All you need to do is bring your computer, planner, and a few files. I've already emailed everything to you."

I blew out a breath of relief, glad he at least sent me a list of what I needed to do before we left. I gathered myself and thanked him for being considerate. "Thank you, sir, but if you don't mind, may I leave a little early to pack?" Hopefully, he understood my need to get organized.

"Remi, I said I took care of everything. You don't need to pack anything except toiletries and the things I sent you in the email. I'll take care of you."

I wasn't sure what "I'll take care of you" meant exactly, but I could take care of myself. The smirk on his face as he spoke those words made me wonder if I was missing something. I watched as he rose from his desk chair to his full height. My head tilted all the way back so I could maintain eye contact with him. He moved around to stand in front of me, leaned down and put his massive hands on my shoulders. "Remi, I want to do this, so let me," he comforted me, massaging my shoulders.

The action almost put me in a trance. His touch was so satisfying. My eyes fluttered closed, and the tension left my body. I was so pliable, I had to force down a moan. When I slowly opened my eyes, I quickly realized I was eye level with his crotch.

Unconsciously, I sighed and licked my lips. He was hard and long, a reaction to the intimacy of the massage. And for a moment, I wondered what it would be like to have him in my mouth. It was as if I was hypnotized. I could feel myself drifting closer, as if on its own accord, needing a taste. The squeezing of my shoulders brought my eyes snapping back to him. And there it was, the desire I'd seen in those bourbon eyes that day a month ago. He wanted me, and right now I wanted him too.

The realization was like a bucket of icy water dumped on my head. I jumped out of my chair, jerking out of his grasp, before I could do something stupid, like come onto my boss. His hands fell to his sides reluctantly. I had broken the spell. I'd quickly come to my senses.

"Can I go?" I cleared my throat because even I could hear the breathlessness in it. "Sir, I have a lot to do."

He agreed, tipping his head to one side as if studying me, then a quick nod. I booked it out to his office and down the hall to mine so fast, I was out of breath. I slammed my door and retreated to my chair. Resting my head on top of my hands on the desk, I tried to figure out what the hell just happened. I almost assaulted my boss.

"Damn it!" Frustrated, I pounded my fist on my desk, just to focus on something other than Mr. St. Clair.

I took a deep breath and began gathering my things. I had a long week ahead of me, and I couldn't afford distractions. And fantasizing about sucking my boss's dick was definitely a distraction. The meeting this week was important to St. Clair Technologies. I had to put all of my emotions behind me and make sure it was a success. More determined than ever to do a splendid job as usual, I headed for the elevator and home for the evening.

CHAPTER SIX

When I got home, I didn't even bother with my usual routine. Normally, I came into my apartment, dropped my things on my couch, and just sat for a minute or two with my eyes closed just to unwind. But tonight called for something a little more potent. I went straight to my wine rack and pulled out my last bottle of Rossi.

My bag, with my planner and computer, slumped to the floor as I plopped into a dining room chair. I unwrapped the top and pulled at the cork until it popped out the bottle into my hand. I didn't even bother with a glass. I'm usually more civilized than that, but I just tipped the bottle up to my lips and took a long, satisfying swig. Rarely did I drink at home, it had to be a special occasion like dinner with my neighbors or Erica was over for a girls' night, and I most *certainly* didn't drink from the bottle. Perfectly good wine glasses that read "Bitches Be Sippin'" I had ordered from a random website as a gag gift and decided to keep were just in the cabinet. By the time my nerves were calm and I could think somewhat clearly, it was almost nine, my usual bedtime, the bottle was half empty, and I had packed nothing.

I pushed the cork back onto the Rossi, twisting the wires to hold it in place, and put it in the fridge, then headed to my room to pack. "Whoops," I belted out as I ran slam into the wall to the right of me. I guess I was a little tipsy. Shrugging, I giggled as I made it to my room and sat on my bed to stop the world from spinning.

I didn't even know what to bring, so I just grabbed a week's worth of underwear and outfits. If we stayed longer, I'd just buy something while I was there. Mr. St. Clair said to only pack toiletries, that he would take care of everything, but I didn't want him to spend any money on me no matter how much he had. I didn't want to owe him anything. I zipped the suitcase, rolled it to the door, and headed back to the living room. I sat on my couch and flicked on the TV when my phone screamed out. It was loud as hell, or I was forming a headache from the wine I drank. I checked the caller ID. It was Erica. I had been drowning in my own panic so much, I'd forgotten to call her and tell her I was leaving work early because of my trip.

"Hello." I pushed out a sigh.

"Well, hello to you, too. I came by your office before I left. You weren't there."

"Yeah, I'm sorry. I had to come home and pack. Time got away from me."

"Wait, what do you mean pack?"

I could hear rustling in the background, indicating she was getting comfortable as she awaited my story. I tried to get comfortable too. The wine had a mellowing effect. I finally pulled off my shoes and walked over to the fridge for the ice cream I'd bought last week and hadn't touched. I guessed this was better than drinking the rest of that Rossi and giving myself a hangover. I didn't want to risk being late in the morning. I pulled a spoon out of the dish drainer and settled into the couch. As I ate my ice cream, I relayed the details of my meeting with Mr. St. Clair. I debated whether to tell Erica about my mental lapse, lusting over our boss's dick. But in the end, I decided I couldn't *not* tell her. I took a deep breath and stilled myself as I told her about our intimate moment.

"Damn it, I knew it!" came over the receiver, and I pulled it away from my ear because Erica was practically yelling.

I put her on speaker before my eardrums burst. I couldn't pig out on my ice cream and hold my phone at the same time anyway. "Shit, Erica. Stop screaming," I growled as I swallowed my spoonful of ice cream. She was excited, and to be honest, for the love of God, her enthusiasm had my drunk ass giddy too.

"I knew there was something going on between you two," she clapped triumphantly.

I almost choked on my ice cream trying to correct her. "Erica, there is *nothing* going on. I am sure every single woman, and probably some married women too, fantasize about him. Even you were saying how *yummy* he was the other day." I rolled my eyes even though she couldn't see me. Maybe I should've drunk the rest of that wine.

Her laughter came over the line as she reiterated her summation of him. "Girl, he *is* yummy. Those designer suits and that beard do it for me." She laughed even harder. I couldn't help but to join in as she continued to objectify our boss. "That shiny bald head glistening between your legs, just hold on and enjoy the orgasm."

Feigning disgust, I laughed. "Eww…Erica! You're a mess," I chastised.

"What?! I'm telling the truth. I bet he could bring a woman to orgasm with a flick of his tongue."

We chatted for another twenty minutes as she rattled off her plans for the upcoming week. I was going to miss our morning coffees, but I'm sure we would make up for it when I got back. By the time I took my shower and finally laid my body down, it was midnight, and I needed to get up around four in the morning to make sure I wasn't late. When my head hit the pillow, I was pulled into the darkness of sleep.

The next morning, I managed to make it to the airport on time. I was traveling in my first private jet. I was glad I'd thrown my bag together the night before because time was pressing. When I arrived at the tarmac, Mr. St. Clair was there waiting. He paid for my *Lyft* and then helped me out of the car. I hesitated, eyeing his outstretched hand as he encouraged me to get out the vehicle.

"Remi, we don't want to be late," he said, smiling down at me. It was that *I'm-gonna-melt-your-panties-off* kind of smile that I'm sure every woman fell for, but not this woman. But I reluctantly took his hand and let him usher me toward the plane, while someone grabbed my bag out of the trunk.

"How about a grand tour?"

My head bobbed up and down as I took in the surrounding luxury. You couldn't help but gawk at the opulence of this jet. *What did I expect, though?* This was the CEO and Founder of St. Clair Technologies. This man was a billionaire ten times over and had been for most of his adult life. Of course, the jet reflected it. I was wide-eyed as we moved from room to room. A bedroom, full bath and kitchen, all nestled in the back of the plane. The seating area consisted of eight seats grouped in fours around two tables with a full bar. A yawn interrupted his declaration of me making myself at home.

He chuckled, and the sound flowed through my body like a bomb. "Am I boring you Remi?" he inquired as we settled into our seats when the captain asked us to buckle up.

"No, I'm not awake yet," I admitted. "I had a long night of ice cream and my best friend." I smiled, looking over to see he had a grin on his face. I think I liked this side of Mr. St. Clair.

Gotta be because he's able to relax, I guessed. I couldn't imagine running a vast conglomerate like St. Clair Tech.

Seemingly understanding, he agreed. "Believe me, I understand about late nights. Well, you can have the bed in the back if you want to sleep. We have a few hours before we get to Chicago," he offered. At first, I refused. However, I conceded and sleep finally consumed me.

I awakened to the smell of bacon and eggs. I lay there for a few moments, trying to gather my wits because I'd forgotten where I was and how I'd got there. "Wait! How did I get here?" I threw the blanket off, and his cologne embraced me as it lingered in the air.

He carried me?

"There's no way," I surmised, but then thought back to his powerful body and broad shoulders. I'm over two hundred pounds. A shiver racked my body when I realized he had no problem with my weight. It made me wonder what else he could do with my legs wrapped around his waist. I rolled my eyes, "Girl, hush, there's no way we are going there," I declared.

I made my way toward the aromas making my stomach growl, an insistent reminder I hadn't eaten this morning. As I entered the cabin, I saw Mr. St. Clair sitting in front of a full spread. He greeted me as soon as his eyes locked with mine. The right side of his mouth curled up into a sexy smirk as I approached, pointing to the lavishness.

"Sit down," he offered. "Have some."

"So, this is why you wanted the chef. I wondered what the deal was," I grinned, sitting down to fill my plate. I couldn't choose, so I added a little bit of everything I saw. This chef was a five-star one, and the presentation of the food was spectacular. Crepes drizzled in syrup and chocolate with whipped cream topped with slivers of strawberries. Link sausages and the crispiest bacon. It was all almost too pretty to eat.

"I like what I like. Besides, the food's delicious. You've outdone yourself, Remi."

A companionable silence fell over the cabin as we both ate

our fill. All too soon, we were interrupted when the captain's announcement to buckle up came over the speaker as we were about to make our descent.

"Already? You let me sleep a long time," I exclaimed as I took my seat, not believing how long I slept.

"You were tired."

"Yes, I was. I can't seem to get Erica off the phone when she starts in." I chuckled as I think back to all the silliness we discussed last night.

As soon as we touched down, he asked the stewardess to bring our bags. He pulled me up out of my seat, then rested his hand on my lower back as he followed me down the steps. We disembarked a few moments later to an awaiting limo. The driver opened my door, and I settled into the massive interior of lavishness. Mr. St. Clair headed around the other side, waving off the driver as he tried to open his door.

"I've never been in a limo before or a private jet, for that matter." Wonder laced my words as I tried to absorb everything. The rich aroma of black leather seats filled the back of the limo. I inhaled deeply, relishing the scent. I loved the smell of leather. The windows were tinted a coal black. I could see out, but I was pretty certain no one could see in. A partition went up in front of us, as soon as the car started forward, giving us more privacy. He poured two drinks from a bar I hadn't noticed before. The woodgrain shone brightly in the limo's overhead lighting. I reached for mine saying, "Thank you." And took a sip. Probably the best Mimosa I'd ever had because I'm sure the alcohol was top-notch.

"I'm glad you're enjoying it." That smirk formed on his face again, and his cognac eyes sparkled. He nestled back into the leather beside me, causing our knees to briefly touch one another. I couldn't help myself and reciprocated his smile. This was the most open and relaxed I'd ever seen him, and it made me think maybe he wasn't so bad after all.

Within twenty minutes, we arrived at the hotel. I waited for my door to open, watching Mr. St. Clair get out and move around to my door. To my surprise, he waited, being the perfect gentleman, to help me out instead of the driver. This time, I readily took his hand as he gently pulled me from the car. We walked into the lobby. My forward momentum stopped as I was floored at the elegance of the hotel. The pictures on the internet did *not* do it justice. It was *gorgeous*.

"You have a seat while I check in." He began making his way to the front desk before I could even move.

"But, Mr. St. Clair, that's a part of my job," I protested, trying to grab his arm. "This isn't a vacation. I'm here to work," I declared, heading straight to the counter. The desk clerk smiled at me, indicating with a nod of her head that she would be with me in a moment. His body heat rolled off him and seeped into me as he hovered over my shoulder, waiting.

"May I help you?" she asked with a bubbly smile.

I smiled back and rattled off Mr. St. Clair's information along with the confirmation number I pulled up on my phone from my email. The tapping on the keyboard echoed through the lobby.

"I have your reservation, top floor. Here are your keys to the private elevator." I took the two keycards from her. "The number is 1530, the penthouse," she stated with a smile.

"Thank you so much." I turned with the keys to 1530 but realized she'd forgotten the other room. "Wait, I booked two rooms." I turned back in a rush, aware Mr. St. Clair was still watching and listening.

She typed furiously on the keyboard, shaking her head, rechecking her information. "I only have the one room," she reiterated.

"I'm positive I booked two rooms," I protested. I was fantastic at what I did for Mr. St. Clair, but at the moment, her finding only the one room didn't bode well for me. The screwup made me look incompetent. "Can I speak with a manag—?" A firm squeeze of my shoulder halted my request. Mr. St. Clair's body was looming over mine like an ominous cloud.

"The one room is fine, thank you," he interrupted my request, took the keys and pulled me toward the private elevator. He flashed the key in front of a panel, and the doors opened for us. The doors encased our bodies along with my disappointment. I'd never in my entire time working for this man made a mistake like this. I was in disbelief. I pulled out my phone and checked the email sent to me once again. Right there in black and white, it read I reserved two rooms.

"Don't worry about it." His thundering voice circulated around me. When I searched his face, there was a softness in his eyes.

He's not upset.

Relief swept over me, helping lower my stress level. However, there was a need to apologize for the mix-up. "Mr. St. Clair, I'm so sorry. I don't know what happened, but I can assure you it won't happen again," I vowed.

He waved off my apology. "It's fine, Remi. I forgive you."

I was grateful he was taking my fuck-up well because even though he'd been an asshole for as long as I had worked for him, I genuinely loved my job. I didn't want this to cost me. The elevator dinged, indicating we'd reached our floor.

CHAPTER SEVEN

The elevator opened, and Remi's mouth fell open, and her eyes widened. Her reaction warmed my heart so much so that I yearned to see her like this all the time. "Go ahead, look around. Here, let me take your jacket and bag."

The curtains were open. Remi immediately made her way to the windows to see the view. The light filtering through made it seem as if there was a glow surrounding her as she enjoyed the river flowing past our hotel. Returning from putting her bag and jacket in the room, I made my way toward her. "It's beautiful, isn't it?"

"Yes." She didn't make eye contact. Her eyes were trained on the river below.

She was relaxing.

Good.

As I stood beside her, I was hyperaware of my shoulder touching her shoulder as we both enjoyed the water. I wanted to touch her more but restrained myself. The need to woo her first was most important if she was to trust me.

Our bodies disconnected as I moved toward the bar. The

audible release of breath from Remi confirmed she felt the attraction, too. "Do you know the history behind the Chicago River?" I asked, wanting her to release the tension she was still carrying because of the room mishap.

The truth about the rooms was forthcoming, but not yet.

"No, I don't," she admitted.

I presented what I knew about the area as I finished pouring our drinks and moved back to the window. "Well, from what I've read, Chicago became a booming town. The problem was that it didn't have a proper sewage system. That nice calm, clear water you see flowing out there." I pointed to the river. "Was full of sludge from the industries that were up and down this river."

She listened intently, nodding every once in a while but not interrupting me.

"That sludge was flowing into the city's source of drinking water," I informed. "Lake Michigan." She looked out toward the river as I explained.

"How did they clean it up?"

"They redirected the flow of the river." Her eyes stretched. I could see the questions in them. Unexpectedly, I had captured her mind, which hopefully would help capture her heart. I continued the history of the river, her curiosity fueling the story. "Sometimes the river turns green," I spun from the window to sit on the couch. Remi followed me, settling in. I have to admit, even though this was a business trip and "not a vacation," as she put it, it was nice not being in a room alone. I'd had so many of these trips over the years where the silence in the room was so deafening, I hated being there. "It's been a tradition since the sixties," I continued. "They do it for the St. Patrick's Day Parade."

"I didn't know that. This is my first trip to Chicago. New York is the only other state I've been besides North Carolina."

She relaxed against the back of the couch before I'd finished the story. The tension was finally leaving her shoulders. I *wanted* her to make this trip a vacation. She deserved it. I recognized the work she did for me, so showering her was the least I could do.

"We have dinner reservations at seven," I informed her as I headed back to the bar for a refill. "In the meantime, take in some sights or rest. There is time for shopping on the Magnificent Mile if you want. It's up to you," I offered as I poured another drink to occupy myself because if I didn't, I was going to jump the gun on my plans. I offered her a drink. The two I had had were helping me relax, maybe it would do the same for her.

"Please. Thank you."

Another mimosa, she seemed to enjoy the one she'd had in the car.

"But I don't have anything to wear to dinner. I just stuffed work clothes in my suitcase." The panic was starting to take over.

Rushing over, I handed her the drink. She had not moved from the couch, but she was sitting right on the edge about to protest going to dinner with me. "Remi, I said I'd take care of you. So let me." I caressed her cheek. She leaned into my hand, then jerked away as if her skin was on fire. I gestured toward the closed door of the bedroom. "In the closet."

"You bought me clothes!" she yelled.

I was amused by her outburst but knew if I laughed right then, she'd be defensive, so I tried my best to calm her down.

"Yes, I bought you some clothes. It's not a big deal," I tried to convince her. "I just wanted to show you how much I appreciate you coming with me last minute," I rushed out. My explanation seemed to appease her, and I released a breath. *This might be harder than I thought.* I watched anxiously as she cautiously made her way to the bedroom door. After years of being a jerk to her, I didn't blame her for her skepticism. I sat at the counter, sipping my whiskey, wondering what I was going to do about the woman I'd been obsessing over for the past few months.

My mind wandered back to yesterday in my office. I remembered how she reacted to my touch when I revealed she would have to come here with me. I fucking alarmed her that day, but I was only trying to help. I could see my laying the last-minute trip on her frazzled her. She was having a full-on anxiety attack. But when I touched her, it was all I could do not to bring her closer to me and kiss her. She felt so fucking good. Her skin was soft and smooth. It was rare Remi wore her arms and shoulders out. And if she did, they're encased in a blazer. She always looked professional and put together, even though I would like to see her clothes more form fitting for my own selfish reasons.

But I couldn't help myself. As soon as we were skin to skin, my dick woke up. Every caress made it twitch. And when she let out that soft moan, it was all I could do not to come in pants like an eager teenager. Thing was, she kept surprising me the more I watched her. I didn't expect her to open her eyes and caress my dick with her gaze. Her licking her lips was my undoing. I imagined them wrapping around my dick, her tongue licking the length of it and taking it into her mouth again. I wanted that with every fiber of my being, but me pushing my dick inside of Remi in my office wasn't the right time. I had to get her to trust me first, then make Remi McMillan mine. The only woman for months who has been a constant in my head. Since that night at the bar, she was the only woman I wanted in my bed.

I'd made plans to make this trip to Chicago the best she has ever had in her life. I would do whatever it took to make it happen. I was infatuated with her, and I won't rest until I have her. There was no doubt this trip would make that happen.

CHAPTER EIGHT

I made my way to one of the closed doors beyond the living room, just standing there taking in everything. The luxury, the obvious money spent, was becoming overwhelming. It was a beautiful suite, complete with a sitting area, and fireplace. The room was decorated in shades of blue and gray. Only a glimpse of the bathroom assured me it was as lovely as the rest. The walk-in closet in the corner of the room was filled with clothes. I rummaged through them all. Gowns, business attire, jeans, beautiful blouses with matching shoes. I didn't have to check if they were my size. I just knew. Mr. St. Clair was efficient. I bet if I pulled out the top drawer of the dresser snuggled in the back of the closet, there would be lingerie as well.

I chose a simple black dress with spaghetti straps and the nude heels placed under it to wear to dinner. They would look fantastic together. I hung the dress back on the closet rack. I didn't understand why he'd done this. He had claimed it was appreciation, but he could've just bought flowers or something.

I sighed and made my way out of the closet and back into the living room where he was sitting at the bar, with his back to me.

He divested the suit jacket, showing off those strong, broad shoulders. His thick stature made me curious to know if he was that way all over. "But never mind that." Mumbling and shaking my head, I tried to clear it from the unnatural thoughts I was having. His muscles tensed as I refused the clothes. "I can't accept those clothes in there."

He didn't turn around or speak. His silence assured me that he was pissed. I slowly stepped closer to him, inching my way forward until I could reach out and grab his shoulder. Hoping he would focus his attention on me. His muscles twitched beneath my touch, causing me to linger. I resisted the urge to run my hand down his back, just so I could feel it rippling beneath my fingertips.

"Miss McMillan, if you don't stop touching me, I'll fuck you right on this counter."

His husky voice had tingles running through me as his warning was clear. I couldn't help myself and almost called him on his bluff because his declaration made me wet as hell. My pussy fluttered, ready for him. Nevertheless, I removed my hand like his body was a flame, and I didn't want to get burned. So I took a few deep breaths and several steps back. I had become a scared and confused teenager retreating to the room, firmly closing the door behind me. He helped me make my choice to rest instead of shop before our dinner. There was no way I would make it through that time without jumping his bones. The bed was calling my name, and I gratefully heeded and bent to its will. It took several minutes for my heart to return to its normal rate. While my body recovered, I stared at the ceiling, completely mentally drained. This was going to be one hell of a trip if I couldn't get my desires reeled in. Exhaustion, however, won, and I finally drifted off to sleep.

I awoke to my phone shrieking.

It's probably Erica.

But it was already five thirty, and I didn't have the time to answer all the questions she was going to throw my way. So, I ignored it.

I felt like a charity case or something as I pulled the black dress from the closet I'd decided upon earlier, along with a matching bra and panty set from the dresser.

"Figured they would be lace," I mumbled as I held them up to examine them, then threw them on the bed. The dress was very stunning in an understated way. I sighed, resigning myself to just give in to what he wanted for now. I mean, what girl wouldn't go crazy over a closet full of clothes? They all had tags on them, bought especially for me.

Walking into the bathroom to draw a bath, I noted how opulent the whole thing was. Black slate on the floor and walls. A glass shower, complete with a sitting bench. The tub was big enough for three people, I observed as I undressed.

"It's nice to finally get out of those travel clothes."

The place was stocked with oils, salts, and bath balls. The lavender and lemon-scented oil flowed into the water, and I lowered myself in. I'd never been this pampered before in my life. As the stresses of the day melted away, relaxing for over an hour was very tempting, but there wasn't enough time. Reluctantly, I made myself step out of the tub and grab one of the fluffy black robes hanging on the back of the door. I had enough time to get dressed, but unfortunately, I couldn't dawdle in the luxuriousness of my surroundings.

The way my life was set up, if I didn't start now, I was sure something would go wrong. I tackled my hair first, spraying water and putting in my favorite product. I pinned the unruly curls up into a bun. Small tendrils tickled my bare neck. Appreciation for what I saw staring back at me in the vanity mirror made the small smile I sported on my lips swell. My makeup was light. I'd never been one to wear a full face often. My normal look consisted of tinted moisturizer, eyeliner, a bit of mascara, and lip gloss—you could never have enough lip gloss. I slid the applicator over my full bottom lip once more, then smacked my lips together. "There. Done." I was pleased with what I saw looking back at me.

Finally, I slipped the matching lingerie on. The gorgeous black dress pulled up right over my hips. The convenience of this dress having no zipper was a plus. My feet settled into the nude heels effortlessly. They looked good on me. I made my way to the full-length mirror near the window to admire my work. I wish I'd brought jewelry. My diamond earrings from my mother would set this look off. In my haste, I'd forgotten them at home. My cell phone rang again. I never called Erica back. She would just keep calling if I didn't answer, but I couldn't dedicate the time to start a conversation with her. It would be hours before I was able to even hang up.

Declined.

"I'll call her tomorrow."

I took one last look in the full-length mirror. "This is as good as it's gonna get," I uttered and started out of the room. A note I hadn't noticed before on the desk by the door caught my eye. I opened it and held the square box it was attached to. The other covered my mouth as I read.

REMI,

I KNOW THIS IS UNEXPECTED, BUT PLEASE WEAR THESE AS A TOKEN OF MY APPRECIATION. YOU'RE LOVELY INSIDE AND OUT. THE CAR WILL BE THERE AT SIX THIRTY.

TONY

Nestled inside the black box was the most beautiful set of diamond earrings and necklace I'd ever seen. My hands trembled as I removed the necklace first. I swore it took me three times to get it on because they were shaking badly. Then the earrings. They were larger carat than the ones my mother gave me. Their weight was heavy on my lobes. My head turned from side to side, admiring the glint they gave off in the waning evening sun coming through the window.

I appreciated the gift, but time was closing in. With fifteen minutes remaining before I left, I explored the rest of the penthouse. I wanted to see what this place had to offer. Not only had I never ridden in a private jet or a limo, but I'd never stayed in a luxury hotel, let alone a penthouse suite.

Every closed door was explored. There was a coat closet, the gym Mr. St. Clair insisted upon, a guest bathroom, and sliding doors leading to the balcony and Jacuzzi.

"What the hell?" I pirouetted, making sure I hit every door in the suite. "There's no second bedroom."

By the time I made a second round through the penthouse, my anxiety was at the highest level, and I was out of time to think about our sleeping arrangements. Rushing to the elevator, I paused to take several deep breaths before my heart exploded out of my chest. By the time I hit the lobby, I realized the deep breaths weren't working. My stress would have to be released another way, preferably in a suite of my own. Just as the note stated, the car was waiting for me at six thirty sharp. The driver opened my door. With the driver's help, I slid inside. The woodgrain beckoned me, and I was going to heed its call.

The bar.

"Thank you because I need a drink or two to get through this week if there's only one bed," I muttered, pouring myself a stiff one.

CHAPTER NINE

There she was.

I spotted her as soon as she made her way toward me following the hostess. She looked sensational in the dress I'd purchased for her. I made a guess on her size, but it was clear I did well. I grinned as I spied the diamond necklace around her neck and the earrings I purchased for her as well, donning her skin. I was pleased she didn't put up a fuss about them as she did the clothes.

We had a private dining area at the back of one of the many excellent restaurants on the Magnificent Mile. This was just the start. Maybe one night this week, we'd use that five-star chef I had Remi hire for me. The food he prepared on the jet was succulent. The restaurant boasted an amazing floor-to-ceiling panoramic view of Lake Michigan on its website, and it delivered everything it promised. The view was amazing, even to me, a man who had dined at some of the finest restaurants around the world. But I wanted this to be an experience of a lifetime for Remi, away from the media and prying eyes. I didn't want them to meddle in her life. The media could sometimes ruin everything in this social circle.

There was a slight wobble to her step. It was obvious she hit the bar either in the room or the car. Frown lines marred her lovely face. I wanted to wipe them away, never wanting to see those lines spread across those features again. I rose, smiling, then kissed her on the cheek. The astonishment from my actions replaced that frown. Her eyes were wide, and her lips slightly opened. I placed my palm on her lower back, helping her get seated. Then I took mine.

"There's only one room," she slurred, not wasting time with small talk.

I cleared my throat. I knew this would come up. She must've looked around the place when she woke from her nap.

"Yeah." I shrugged. "I can take the couch."

She needed to sober up for this conversation, so I poured her a glass of water from the carafe left at our table. I guess the "craft a cocktail" experience I added to our dinner was out of the question now. Her glass paused halfway to her lips, and I couldn't help but fantasize about kissing them. She put the glass down.

"Why can't we just get another room?"

It was logical for her to ask, but I expected that question. "I tried already, while you were asleep."

I waited for more questions. Hopefully, she would just take my word for it. In order for my plan to succeed, I need Remi to be in the same room as me. Relieved when she didn't ask any, I assured her things would work out. "It'll be fine."

As our food arrived, I canceled the "cocktail experience," vowing we would be back to participate another day this week. I glared pointedly at Remi when I spoke and ordered a bottle of wine.

She looked down at her hands in her lap bashfully. "I'm sorry, I had a little too much to drink on the ride over," confirming what I'd already suspected.

"I took the liberty of ordering for you, so we wouldn't have to wait. I hope you like it."

"What is it?" The question swam in her sparkling dark brown eyes. They looked to be almost black.

"Remi, I promise you it's not poisoned." The waiter sat my skirt steak in front of me, minus the brussels sprouts. I didn't care for those. The glimpse of suspicion on her face had me chuckling. I couldn't help myself. I motioned to her plate with my fork. "That's Mafaldine. You'll love it. I promise. It's one of several excellent pasta dishes they have."

The restaurant boasted a five-star chef, so the dishes were top-notch. She finally picked up her silverware, picking at the tomatoes on her plate. I was surprised but relieved when she dug in with such gusto.

We ate as companions. She didn't seem too open about talking about her life when I asked her why she moved to New York. I didn't want to push, and instead I shared the story of my childhood.

"Well, let's see. I'm the typical rags to riches story, I guess. We lived in a small two-bedroom house, my parents and me. It was a tough neighborhood, but we stuck together. My parents were strict, so I couldn't hang in the streets like a lot of my friends did from school."

"In by the time the streetlights came on?" A grin flitted across her face as if she had the same experience.

"You got it. A lot of the kids from the neighborhood teased me about it, so you can imagine the fights I got into." Now it was my turn to grin as I remembered my mom fussing because I chose to fight instead of running away. "I was such a trouble for my parents." I took another bite of my steak before continuing, "It was school, practice or games depending on which sport's season was in, and then home. After me, my mom couldn't have any more kids, so I was an only child. A loner for sure until I met Ashley."

"Who's Ashley?" The curiosity and maybe a hint of jealousy swirled there in her eyes, laced in her voice. Inside, I was smirking because no other woman compared to her in my eyes.

"She's my best friend," I explained. "We met in the seventh grade. She and her family moved into the house next door to us." I took a bite of my steak and washed it down with the wine. "She saw me outside playing basketball in the yard, came over to play, and ever since then, we have been tight with one another."

I took another sip of wine. "Every once in a while, we'll catch a movie, go to a bar. She keeps me grounded and from getting a big head."

"I can understand that. I don't have anyone from home I'm that close to." Her shoulders sagged a little as she revealed her loneliness to me. "But I thank God every day for Erica." The brightest smile lit her face as she spoke about her friend.

I thought back to the female I saw her with on more than one occasion as well as at the bar that night. Somehow, knowing she had a close friend to confide in and do things with, gave me comfort. "Anyway, I discovered I had a talent for electronics. I had a small laptop. About a thirteen-inch screen, it was slower than a turtle and no memory whatsoever. But it was all my parents could afford, just to do schoolwork on. One day it started acting crazy," I chuckled and shook my head because at that age that was how I described it, "I took it apart, basically rebuilt it. After that, anything that had anything to do with tech I was diving in. Went to college, and the rest is history."

Just then, her cell phone rang. She removed it from her clutch to check the ID. The frown lines were back again when she declined the call and dropped the phone back into her purse.

"Is everything all right?" I didn't want to be too forceful, it was really none of my business, but I didn't want anything to ruin our night either. She was silent for a moment and then plastered a smile on her face, although it didn't quite meet her eyes.

"No, I'm fine," she assured me.

She pushed her plate away. Frustration overcame me because I could see whoever was on the line had completely fucked up her night.

"Are you sure?" I implored. I wanted her to tell me who it was. But I didn't want to revert to the ass she thought I was. The tension had settled in my shoulders. I was pissed because she was upset, and there was nothing I could do about it because she didn't trust me enough yet.

She giggled a little, and I relaxed somewhat. "Mr. St. Clair."

I interrupted her, "Please call me Tony. I insist."

"Tony." She hesitated, as if she was testing how my name rolled off her tongue. To me, it was like music. I longed to hear her whisper my name as I was fucking her, to scream it as she climaxed. "I'm going to the restroom," she said, getting up from her chair. "I think the alcohol and water have finally hit me."

I dipped my head once, not insisting anymore. It was obvious to me she didn't want to share with me what was bothering her. I rose from my seat as she rushed away from the table. "Well, this is turning to shit," I muttered, my eyes following Remi's retreat.

The waiter returned to our table to rid us of the empty plates and to refill our drinks. "Leave the wine and bring an order of tiramisu, please." The piece was sizable enough for two people, so we could share it. He affirmed he heard my order before scurrying off toward the kitchen.

My eyes wandered to the restroom area of the restaurant when Remi was taking longer than I thought necessary. Then again, most women took forever in there, or at least the ones I knew. I was just glad she didn't have anyone to go with her, then she would never leave. I snickered at my tasteless joke, genuinely worried about Remi. I needed her to not see her boss when she looked at me. I was not going to lie. I wasn't taking no for an answer. She would be mine. I had a laser focus when it came to her. The infatuation I had for Remi was becoming something more. An obsession, perhaps? Oh, absolutely. An obsession I didn't intend to let go of.

When she returned from the restroom, she looked even more frazzled than when she went in. Her cell buzzed again, but this time it was three text messages back-to-back-to-back. She didn't even bother responding to them and just put it on vibrate. Her foul mood had to do with those calls and texts I bet.

After a little more wine, small talk about what to expect tomorrow at the meeting ensued, and we enjoyed some of the delicious tiramisu then left the restaurant. I'd planned to take her to enjoy the city lights, a short walk to help with digestion, but I could see she was not up for it. Plus, we had a big day tomorrow. This meeting was important for my company, and I didn't want anything to affect the outcome.

"You ready to go back to the hotel?" I asked as I slipped into the car after her and closed my door.

She suppressed a yawn. I smiled, at least she didn't seem worried anymore, but I could see the jetlag creeping in on her. I told the driver to head back to the hotel. The ride was pleasant, but the day was wearing on Remi. The motion of the car was the perfect lull for sleep. She rested her head on the back of the seat and closed her eyes, not yet asleep. And I didn't blame her. I was a little tired myself.

By the time we got to the room and Remi settled in the bedroom, a wave of exhaustion was settling in on me as well. I was elated to sit on the couch that would be my bed for, hopefully, only one night. I closed my eyes for a second to unwind, but I could sense her standing over me. I cracked my eye open. Damn, she was still beautiful, even with the noticeable strain around her eyes.

"I thought you were going to bed," I said, pulling off my suit jacket and loosening my tie.

She sat beside me, folded her legs up into the couch, and flicked on the TV. She wore a tank and threadbare pajamas. Her long curls were in a high ponytail. "I couldn't sleep," she continued, surfing the channels until she settled on a romantic comedy. I pulled my shoes off and lifted my feet onto the coffee table to get comfortable. It was only nine, but it seemed as if it was midnight. My body was just weary. "Why did you do all this?"

The question was unexpected and out of nowhere. My breath hitched for a second. I thought she was referring to the cancellation of the other room. That she had found out somehow and was just mentioning it. But there was no way she could know about that. When her hand flitted toward the room and the open closet, I understood what she meant. "I wanted to show my appreciation. You do an expert job, Remi. I understand I'm not the easiest person to work for." She didn't question me, but I could see her mind churning as if she wanted to probe more. But she didn't say anything more and turned back to the TV.

The movie was not my style, but she seemed to enjoy it. Her eyes sparkled with tears at the sad scenes, and a smile always hovered at the corners of her mouth because of the jokes. I grabbed her ankles and draped them across my lap. She drew them up and gave me a wary glance. "Just give them here. Your ankles are swollen." I blew out a breath of exasperation because she still had no faith in me. I had a plan for that, though. This week would be about her and getting her to fall for me. I rubbed her feet, and just touching her skin had electricity shooting through my body.

Did she sense it too?

I glanced at her when a moan escaped her lips. It was the sexiest thing I'd ever had the pleasure of hearing. I wanted her to do it again as I was balls deep inside her. I tamped my fire down because this was about her and worked my way up her calves. I didn't go any further, just continued my ministrations.

The room seemed still and quiet, even with the din of the movie in the background. My focus was solely on Remi and her comfort. Suddenly, her cell blared again. She grabbed it up from the table and turned it completely off. Again, I didn't ask. Best believe I wanted to, but I had to respect her space and privacy, hoping eventually she would feel comfortable enough to tell me. To date, there was very little I knew about Remi's personal life, and she divulged little over dinner. She didn't say whether or not she had a significant other, and I prayed like hell she didn't. But if so, that relationship was over. I'd make sure of that. Focusing once again on her ankles, I slowly moved up her calves. I worked my hands up, down, and around her muscles.

Soon her breathing slowed, and her head rested on the cushion. I maneuvered myself, careful not to jostle her when I placed her feet down onto the floor and scooped her up from the couch. I headed to the bedroom and laid her gently on the bed, like she was the most precious thing in the world.

To me, she was.

I took one last look at her after pulling the blanket at the end of the bed up over her and closed the door softly behind me.

I returned to the living room, heading to the coat closet by the door where the housekeeping staff stocked the extra linens I requested. I made the couch up like a little bed. "Just like Grandma's." I laughed, remembering when my cousins and I had sleepovers at my grandparents' house when our parents were at the club. I was appreciative of the ease of getting comfortable and easily relaxed as sleep took over. We have a full day tomorrow.

CHAPTER TEN

I awakened to the sun blazing into my room through the open curtains I had forgotten to close before I'd left for dinner. The last things I remembered was Mark calling my phone *again* and Mr. St. Clair rubbing my feet before I drifted off to sleep. I stretched, ready to start the day. The smell of coffee drifted into the bedroom. The aroma beckoned me to follow. I didn't even bother turning on my phone because I knew there would be about ten missed calls and just as many texts from Mark.

Why the fuck is he calling me?

I was at a total loss for what was going on in his tiny brain as I scooted to the bathroom to take a quick shower, knowing Mr. St. Clair must be waiting on me. The temptation to stay for another hour or so weighed heavily. The water was tranquil. Questions and concerns about Mark washed down the drain as I allowed myself to bask in the tingle of the water hitting my skin. However, it was already after six, and the meeting with Transient was at eight this morning.

I dressed in one of the outfits I brought with me. They were added to the already packed closet, filled with the clothes Mr. St.

Clair bought for me, last night when I changed. My curls went up into a high ponytail with some light makeup. Grabbing my phone off the bedside table, I reluctantly turned it on. Just as I suspected, several notifications came through. The majority of them are from Mark and a few from Erica. Like I'd done since he started this mess, I ignored them, but quickly tapped out a reply to Erica:

ME

Hey, chica. I was out of it last night and went to bed early. I'll text you later.

Not waiting for her reply, I meandered out of the bedroom, stopping in my tracks as I saw my boss staring out the floor-to-ceiling windows. He looked content and not the least bit concerned at all about today. He seemed relaxed, standing at his full height. I couldn't help but appreciate his stature as I studied him. And did I mention he's sexy as hell? Mr. St. Clair had always worn his suits well. The custom fit Armani—he had me take his suits to the cleaners a time or two—fitted snug in all the right places, while leaving enough room for him to maneuver his sizable frame.

"Good morning," I announced, moving toward the coffeemaker.

He turned, flashing me those white teeth and his million-dollar smile. It almost stole my breath. I wanted to see that smile on his face every day. He mostly wore a serious look or one of disappointment at work. I tore away from his beautiful features to doctor my coffee as he finished his orange juice.

"You ready for the meeting?" he asked, setting his glass down on the counter.

"Yes," I confirmed, cognizant of the documents in the folder Mr. St. Clair gave me before I left his office. I had a chance to go through them on my way to the airport. I took two more sips of coffee, poured the rest in the sink and grabbed my bag. His hand braced my lower back as he ushered me to the elevator. I tried not to flinch and instead settled into his touch with a sigh. The warmth of his hand seeped into my skin, causing me to unwind. I shouldn't have relished it, but I did.

I am in so much fucking trouble.

The ride to Transient Technologies was brief. And in that short amount of time, Mark had called me twice. And I had ignored his call twice. Mr. St. Clair didn't acknowledge he was curious about the calls, but I caught his glare every time my phone rang. I found myself wanting to explain but thought better of it. We weren't *together*, I didn't have to explain anything to him, but I could see it irritated him. The smile was no more, and the sparkle in his hickory brown eyes was now dull.

When we arrived, Mr. Smith's personal assistant met us in the lobby. I watched the man acknowledge Mr. St. Clair with a terse bob of his head, and my boss did the same, but neither man extended their hand to shake.

"This is going to be interesting," I muttered under my breath.

Mr. St. Clair glared at me, hearing my declaration, but didn't respond. My shoulders shook with a silent laugh as we were escorted to a conference room on the top floor of the high-rise building. The view was amazing. You could see a hint of Lake Michigan from where we sat. The windows seemed to be made from the same type of glass as our limo's windows. I was sure no one could see in, but at a hundred and fifty feet, I couldn't imagine why the room would need those types of windows. Mr. Smith was waiting for us and rose as we entered. He was flanked by a woman I assumed to be security. She was standing ramrod straight over his right shoulder with an earpiece in her ear. Same as before, the men nod to one another, no handshakes. It was clear there was no love lost between those two.

"St. Clair," he said, waiting for us to take our seats.

"Smith," Mr. St. Clair acknowledged.

Mr. Smith sat, and I settled in my seat to the right of Mr. St.

Clair. There were others in the room who I assumed were Transient's board and investors.

"Before we start, let me get everyone acquainted," Mr. Smith began, introducing each person sitting at the table. He finally came to the woman standing behind him, "And this is my head of security, Tisha McLean." He pointed at her as she dipped her head.

I could tell Mr. St. Clair was offended by her presence. The frown lines in his forehead had become ever-present since we'd arrived. This was not a hostile takeover. Just a supply and demand situation. Transient had products St. Clair Technology could use. This was just a contract negotiation. So why did it feel like we were about to go to war?

"Security, Steve? Is she really necessary?" he growled.

Mr. Smith took Mr. St. Clair's slight in stride. Leaning back in his executive leather chair, he steepled his hands, contemplating Mr. St. Clair's question. "Tony, you know as well as I do that in this business, it's easy to accumulate enemies. I need protection," he reasoned.

Mr. St. Clair seemed to accept his logic, knowing how Mr. Smith conducted business, and we moved on with the introductions. "This is my personal assistant, Miss McMillan," he motioned to me. I greeted everyone, pulling out my planner to take notes. I had my laptop with me, but it was much easier for me to take the important parts down and type them up later.

There was no waste of time when we got down to business and the negotiations started. I took my notes, being certain to record everything anyone from Transient mentioned. I had to admit though, Mr. Smith was a wily businessman, or maybe he *was* just crooked like I'd heard. On several occasions, he pointed out how St. Clair Technologies needed him, not the other way around, when Mr. St. Clair pushed back on his price. It was lavish to me, but I was just the assistant, and both men had made billions of dollars. My boss was so livid he was about to have a conniption. Several times during the meeting, I placed my hand on his leg and squeezed, trying to calm him down. By eleven, the men had agreed to a number acceptable to both sides. Mr. St. Clair had an ironclad contract for the parts we needed, and Mr. Smith was millions richer.

"I'll meet with my lawyers tomorrow to finalize everything," Mr. St. Clair stated as we made our way to the door. It was amazing to me that with one phone call, his lawyers would meet with him anywhere in the world. Guess that was what money could do for you.

Laughter rang out after us. "Nice doing business with you, Tony," I heard as we stepped into the elevator.

As soon as we were out of the building and into the car, my cell vibrated in my bag. I'd made a habit of turning the ringer off when I was meeting with Mr. St. Clair. He was the type of man who didn't like distractions when he was discussing business.

"Shit," I said, because I knew exactly who it was. I pulled the phone from my bag and answered. "What the fuck do you want?" I pushed out between clenched teeth. "No. No. I can't do this right now," I shouted, hanging up the phone. "Damn it!" I yelled, pissed at myself for even answering the phone. I knew who it was and what he was about. That was why I left him.

How the fuck did he get my number?

The first thing I did when I got to New York was change my number. This was the first time I'd had any contact with Mark in almost four years. What the hell does he want?

"Are you okay?" Mr. St. Clair's deep treble brought me back to reality. I'd forgotten he was there. I didn't trust myself not to break down and cry because I was infuriated. Instead of answering, I just gazed out the window, but my mind was a turbulent thunderstorm. Mr. St. Clair sensed I didn't want to speak about what he'd just witnessed. When he didn't push for answers, I was grateful.

I bolted out of the car and through the lobby before the driver or my boss could open my door. I just wanted to get my work done and forget about the can of worms I opened that comes with Mark. The private elevator had already hit the first floor by the time Mr. St. Clair reached me. I didn't speak, and he didn't either as the doors swooshed open, and we stepped in.

My mind was racing, wondering what Mark had up his sleeve. The ride up was a blur, as I was completely lost in my head. Ducking my head to avoid the questions I was sure my boss had, I stepped past him and into the suite. Mr. St. Clair hovered behind me. His body heat pliant against my body, but he apparently didn't feel the need to bombard me with questions, which was a relief.

I was hard-pressed to get to work to take my mind off Mark. I immediately set up my laptop and transcribed the notes I took during the meeting. They're important in finalizing everything for the contract. And I wanted to make sure Mr. Smith hadn't tried to slip in anything sinister during the negotiations. The action between the two businessmen today was fascinating and simultaneously made me suspicious. The lawyers needed to look over the documents carefully.

Halfway through transcribing the notes, the sensation of being watched took hold of me. With my back to him, his cologne tickled my senses. It was intoxicating, and his presence was distracting me from my work. My body was primed, ready for him. The reaction took me aback. He didn't even touch me, although I wanted him to. I *desperately* wanted him to.

"Get dressed," his deep baritone reverberated through my body, and I was instantly wet. "We have a lunch date," he directed.

I sighed. "I'm really not in the mood, Mr. St. Clair. I just want to finish this so we can get back home," I continued typing the notes. He closed my laptop almost smashing my fingers.

"What the fuck? Why'd you do that?" I was irate and definitely way out of line for speaking to him that way, but he was out of line too. "I don't have time for this," I mumbled, making my way to the room.

He caught my wrist as I tried to skirt past him. "I said get dressed. We're going to Riverwalk." The smile he flashed was his attempt to lessen the cruelty of his demand and his pulling me to the bedroom door. Rummaging through my bag, he pulled out a pair of ripped skinny jeans and a tank top I threw in at the last minute. "And put on some sneakers," he called out, pulling the door closed.

"I didn't bring any sneakers with me," I called out through the closed door.

"Closet," he yelled back.

"Of course, there are sneakers in the closet," I grumbled, stalking over to the closet, dead set on not accepting any of the clothes he'd bought. Growing up, I never asked for beyond what my father could afford. I knew he had a hard time being a single parent, a single dad to a little girl, for that matter. But he did the best he could, and I was good with that. I made it a point not to ask for Jordans and all the other name brands most of the girls at school wore. I was content with my cute sandals or slides from Walmart. Not that I didn't want any of those other things. We just couldn't afford them. So, you could imagine my face when I saw a pair of brand new, still in the box, black Nike Airmax in the corner of the closet. I hadn't even noticed them before. I sat on the bed, dumping the sneakers onto the floor. I was not going to argue with him this time because I did need the walking shoes. I gritted my teeth and hopped in the shower.

CHAPTER ELEVEN

Because the guest bathroom didn't have a shower, I headed to the gym. I couldn't just sit there and watch Remi bury herself in work, trying to cope with whatever shit was going. The episode in the car wired me up. I wanted to punch someone for pulling that reaction from her. Whoever was on the other end of that call sure as hell got on her nasty side.

I took a brief shower, ready to whisk her away for the best time of her life. I wrapped the towel around me and headed for my clothes hanging in the closet. The closet was big enough for both the wardrobe I had stocked for her, as well as my own. Remi was still in the shower, so I carefully opened the door and quickly removed what I needed. Just as I was leaving the room to get dressed in the guest bathroom, her cell rang. I was so fucking tempted to answer it. I shouldn't, but I was curious to know if it was the same fucker who made her upset earlier.

"Fuck it," I reasoned as I pulled on my underwear and rushed over to check her phone. *No name*, I observed, and quickly answered. I was sure it was the person from earlier. A growly

"Hello" met my ears. "Remi, don't you fucking hang up on me again," he hissed.

I was livid. Who the hell did he think he was speaking to her like this?

"Who the hell is this?" I growled back, hoping the fucker came sideways with me. Instead, there was a brief silence on the other end.

"Where the hell is Remi? Why are you answering her phone?" he groused out.

At this point, I was just glad she was still in the shower. I wanted to let this motherfucker know Remi was mine. "Don't worry about where she is. Are you the asshole who keeps calling her?"

He didn't answer. Instead, he demanded to speak to Remi. "Where the fuck is she?"

I was about to fuck with this guy's head. Maybe if he thought she was seeing someone, he would leave her the hell alone. "Leave my girlfriend alone. That's your one warning. Don't fucking call her again," I barked.

He didn't say anything else and hung up just as I heard the water shut off in the bathroom. I committed the number to memory and got out of there as quickly as I could. I didn't want to catch Remi in all her lusciousness because if I was still in that room when she stepped out, I was not gonna be able to control myself. I grabbed my socks and boots and then quietly closed the door behind me, plotting my next move.

An hour later, Remi sauntered out of the room in the tank top and jeans I had laid on the bed for her. I didn't realize they were ripped jeans when I pulled them out of her bag. Her voluptuous shape was on display in those skinnies. Remi was stacked. She had a magnificent body, and there were all kinds of dirty, nasty things running through my mind. I willed my dick to go down and chastised myself for gawking at her. But with the way I wanted her body and my dick deep in her pussy, all the chastising in the world didn't matter. She stood there looking shy and exposed. I tore my eyes from her body and cleared my throat.

"Are you ready to go?"

The smile she gave me was enough to take my breath away. She grabbed her jacket from the back of the couch. "Where are we off to?"

I chuckled as I ushered her into the elevator. "It's a surprise, but it's not far. We'll be able to walk if you want, or we can take the car. It's up to you."

She looked down at her feet as the elevator brought us to a stop, cocking her foot up to show off the sneakers I bought. "I'm glad I have these then. Thank you again."

Winking at her as we made our way through the revolving doors, I assured, "I told you I'd take care of everything."

It was important to me that she had an exceptional time to take her mind off her troubles and to learn things about me.

"Let's take the car. I kinda enjoy being chauffeured around." She giggled. I pulled my cell out, calling for the car, and in no time, we were making our way down Riverwalk.

"This is so beautiful," she gasped as we took a seat at *The Jetty*, an area set aside, a courtyard of sorts, on the Riverwalk, allowing patrons to rest and take in the peace in the middle of the city. The air seemed pure and untainted here. And even though there were people in our vicinity, you could clearly make out the bees buzzing from the many flowers that surrounded us as well as the orchestra of birds singing all around us.

"It is," I agreed, finding it hard to take my eyes away from her to pay attention to the scenery.

It had been a while since I'd just rested. With Remi, I found myself unwinding and letting my guard down. I wanted to ask her about the mystery man, but I didn't think she trusted me enough. I literally saw her body release the tension. While she looked so serene, I was ensnared. I couldn't take my eyes off her. Her face turned upward, drinking in the sun, as her eyes fluttered closed. There was a slight smirk on her lips, which made me smile, too.

"Ahhh..." she sighed, breathing in the fresh air and blowing it out.

As much as I enjoyed watching her bathe in the surrounding nature, there was no time for us to waste. I had so much planned for us. Kayaking, a late lunch, and then some live music. I only did anything like this with Angela, my best friend. Never with a woman I wanted in my life. The other women were just eye candy for photo ops or just for a release. I'd be the first to admit, I fuck, not wine and dine. But Remi had me wanting things I'd never wanted before.

I hated to break up her serenity. "Hey, you ready? We have to go." I rose from my seat and reached for her hand. She grinned, readily taking mine. I pulled her up from the bench and we made our way to *The Cove*. Her face lit up as she realized where we were headed.

"Oh my god!!! Kayaks!"

I belted out an honest to God belly laugh at her giddiness because she was beating the shit out of my arm in her excitement. Before long, we were in a two-man kayak paddling down the Chicago River. She was quiet as people watched while she tried to get the hang of paddling. I tried to coach her through it, but I guess I wasn't a very good coach because we almost tipped over twice, but she was able to control it. This is the most relaxed I've seen Remi in months. I admit some of the fault for the stress lay with me, but I'm trying to change all that. Hell, it was the most relaxed *I'd* been in a long time.

We left our phones in the car to enjoy one another without distractions. That son of a bitch calling her every minute of the day was a damn distraction. It took some convincing, but she finally agreed. I didn't want that dickhead ruining the experience for her. When we got back to the room, and she settled, I was going to run that fucking number and find out where and who that son of a bitch was. After an hour or so, we paddled back because I wanted to make sure we made it to *Island Party* in time.

"You ready for lunch?" I balanced myself on the shore, pulling her forward, then out.

She lost her footing, heading straight for the ground. I reached out and caught her before she hit the ground, wrapping my arms tightly around her waist, bringing her close to me. I didn't dare let her go. I held on tight, and our eyes connected. My eyes dipped down to her mouth. Her lips were plump and luscious. Just a little taste, that's all I wanted.

She had on this strawberry lip gloss that shone, and it smelled delicious. Her face was so close to mine, all I had to do was…*do it!* The next thing I knew was that her lips melded against mine. Her tongue on the seam of my lips asked for entrance. I opened to her, and to my shock, I was kissing Remi. The woman I'd been infatuated with for months was kissing *me*.

The thought excited me. I was in awe of what was happening, but it urged me to take over our kiss. No one else stood on this shore but us. Everything else faded away, the gawkers, those taking pictures of us. Even the catcalls faded, and there was just Remi. I deepened the kiss, catching every moan and groan she released. I hated for it to end but pulled back, savoring that strawberry gloss on my lips and tongue. We were both panting, trying to catch our breath. I was tempted to just take her back to the room and fuck the hell out of her, but I wanted us to finish our day and perhaps our night would end with us together in bed.

CHAPTER TWELVE

"Wow," I uttered as he pulled away from me and grabbed my hand.

The mischievous smirk on his face and desire in his eyes promised me I was in for the most spectacular night of my life. I was eager to ride this man, to try him out. A flash of him fucking me ran through my mind. I wanted to rub myself against him like a cat rubs itself against its owner when it's looking for affection. That's how riled up and ready I was for him. He lifted my chin upward, giving me another soft peck. It was enough to continue the fire he'd stoked.

"There'll be time for that later," he whispered in my ear. "Let's go eat. You'll need your strength." I didn't utter a word, but I caught the innuendo. Afraid the moan I tried to choke down would escape if I did. I could only bob my head as he pulled me down the street toward a bar and grill. We chose to have our late lunch outside under one of the seven domes the winery featured. I was in mesmerized. My mouth fell open as I stared at the plastic-covered spheres usually reserved for larger parties, but being one of the richest men in the world had its perks. Impressed *and* horny. What a combination. We settled in the love seat and placed our orders.

"So, tell me about yourself," he coerced.

There was no shortage of people outright ogling and sneaking looks at Mr. St. Clair. He was world-renowned. But despite his celebrity and the prying eyes, he only had eyes for me. He was interested only in me and what I had to contribute.

I chuckled nervously as I fumbled with exactly what to tell him. I didn't even know where to start. "To be honest, there is nothing to tell."

"I'm sure that's not true," he prodded, sipping his wine as he waited patiently for me to divulge my life's story.

I was gonna need a considerable amount of wine for this. I took a gulp and began. "What is it you want to know?"

His gaze was intense. Before he could notice my blush, I looked away, gathering my composure. This man did things to me. I was sure there would be more moments like this between us. I mean, he wasn't just some man. He was a billionaire bachelor, voted one of the most eligible ones by a magazine, I didn't have time to read. There were pictures taken of him with supermodels on his arm, for Pete's sake! Not only was he a wealthy bachelor, he was fine as hell and way out of my league. I couldn't even believe I was here with him. And the final reason I shouldn't be entertaining *any* of this…he was my boss. We shouldn't even be eating this glorious lunch or having this day out, at least not together. But I pushed the negativity to the back of my mind and tried to enjoy the experience. He interrupted my thoughts when his hand landed on my thigh and gently squeezed.

"Everything."

That one word alone had my panties seeping wetness and me squirming in the love seat, because it meant so much more than what it implied. It made me want to straddle him and grind against him to relieve the pressure where I ached. A shiver ran through my body at the thought. I took a gulp of wine and calming breaths to release the image from my mind.

"Well, let's see. I'm from a tiny town in North Carolina. My father raised me by himself because my mother died when I was ten," I squeezed out past the lump in my throat, trying not to choke up. Even though it was a long time ago, I thought about her every day. I still talk to her, especially when life threw me curveballs. I squeezed my eyes closed, willing the tears not to fall. Tony was patient with me, giving me time to gather my composure. After a few deep breaths, I continued. "I was a nerd in high school and wasn't very popular." Gah, I hated high school. But it was the worst and best time of my life. I became more independent and responsible having to help my dad out, but I was teased relentlessly for not being outgoing and partying. Not to mention, I never wore the name brands anyway. That just wasn't how I was raised. My parents thought name brands were a waste of money.

A smile slowly formed on my face when he said, "No, you, a nerd?" He laughed aloud. "You say that as if you aren't one now."

His smile was almost…*radiant.* To be honest, I wanted to say more crazy things about myself just to keep it there. At work, he was rigid and stiff, mostly all business. But I'd noticed the last few months he had been getting out around his employees. He'd never done that before, choosing to stay in his office and not get personal. I shrugged, brandishing my own smile at his joke about me. "So, how did a small-town girl like you end up in New York, of all places?" The question I'd been dreading to answer for anyone. But honestly, I'd been itching to tell him the truth since Mark had been blowing up my phone, but what was the point? It was not like he could do anything about it. I elected to tell him the truth, just not about Mark.

"Well, after I graduated college, I applied for jobs all over my area, couldn't really find anything, and I wanted to be able to help my dad with his bills. I mean, he put me through school because he didn't want me to be in debt when I graduated. He busted his ass, it's the least I could do."

Our food arrived at that moment, interrupting my autobiography. I dug into what was probably the absolute best hot dog I'd ever had in my life. Hot dogs and wine. I giggled at Mr. St. Clair's choice of drink. I would've preferred a beer.

"Good, isn't it?" he proclaimed around a big bite he'd taken out of his. "Nothing like a Chicago dog."

I could only nod in agreement because, at the moment, I was stuffing my mouth. "So, anyway," continuing once I swallowed. "I talked with my dad about us moving somewhere with greater opportunities for me to find a job. I wanted to use my degree, but to be honest, I would've taken anything," I shrugged, pouring more wine into my now-empty glass.

I took a massive swig to wash the food down. Even though it was a weird combination, the wine was undeniably excellent. I was sure he knew it would be. If the clothes and the jewelry he'd bought me were any indication, he had excellent taste. I glanced up and realized there was a crowd of people gathered outside our bubble. They recognized Mr. St. Clair and were beginning to snap pictures. Our gazes locked, and comically he rolled his eyes at what was happening around us.

"You'll get used to it," he promised. "Now, back to the story. Is that how you ended up in New York?"

Shit, I was hoping he forgot what we were talking about. Leaving the part out about Mark cheating and me just up and leaving, I continued.

"Needless to say, my dad is a Southerner born and raised and refused to come with me. I send him money every month to help out. Of course, he fusses, but I want to do it," I said, picking up my dog and taking the last bite before I resumed my story. "I got lucky with this job. Working for you. But as I said before, I would've taken *any* job."

He leaned forward, reaching his hand toward me. I froze, not able to move an inch because of what his touch did to my body. "I would've hired you, regardless. It's the best thing I have ever done. What would I do without you?" he explained as his thumb wiped something off my cheek.

"Thanks," appreciative of his honest words and attention.

I was not quite able to stare him in the eyes and hoped he was not able to see my red-tinged cheeks. This man was eliciting feelings from me that Mark hadn't in the three years we were together. I chugged the last of my wine as he did, too.

"You ready for some more of this adventure?"

His smile was as genuine and pure as I'd ever seen it. I loved it. And what was worse, I wanted to be the one to keep it there. I didn't know where these emotions were coming from, but I needed to be careful, or I might lose my heart to this man. Allowing him to pull me up out of the love seat, he dropped several bills on the table to pay for our meal and tip. It was close to five, and I couldn't believe we'd been here for almost two hours. I had to admit, though, I was interested in what else he had up his sleeve.

As soon as we stepped out the bubble, we were bombarded by cell phone cameras and people asking for selfies and autographs. To my surprise, he obliged some of them but kept me close to his hip as we pushed our way through the crowd. Thankfully, no one followed us as we continued down Riverwalk.

We walked for several minutes before I started to hear music. I was so excited I began to tug Mr. St. Clair toward it. "You hear that?" The grin on my face was so wide, my cheeks hurt. I was sure my eyes closed just so I could feel the music. He laughed but allowed me to haul him down the walk. We came to a wide-open area where people had blankets, towels, and lawn chairs sprawled out in front of the band playing a set on a small stage. To the right of the stage was an empty section where a few folks were dancing. "Oh my gosh, I love live music," I squealed.

I was like a kid at the state fair my dad used to take me to every year in Raleigh. The night before, I could never sleep because I was always too excited.

Mr. St. Clair pulled me toward two chairs sitting under a vast tree on the outer edge of the clearing, as the band began to play a new song. As soon as we settled, a waitress appeared, handing us two beers before meandering away. "Mr. St. Clair, you planned this, didn't you?" Wonder laced my question. Amazement covered my face. This man kept surprising me. Showing me a different side of him at every turn.

That deep chuckle reverberated through my body and caused my blood to stir. "How many times do I have to tell you to call me Tony," he reiterated. I agreed at his request as the band continued to play. It was almost like they were waiting on us.

"Now, normally, live music is only here from Thursday to Sunday." I grinned as I realized he paid someone for me to have this moment. To be honest, this man had pulled out all the stops today. The question was why? The fuzziness of my brain wouldn't allow me to dwell on it too long. The beers kept coming, and the music was thumping through my body. I could barely contain myself in my seat. I wanted to dance. He smirked my way as I wiggled and moved to the beat of the drums. "Go ahead." He uttered, nodding toward the dance floor, giving me his permission.

Passing him my beer, I hopped out of my seat and made my way to the makeshift dance floor. My hips swayed, fueled by the alcohol. I felt alive, fresh, and free. Nothing was bringing me down. My arms went up over my head. My hands reached for the sky. My eyes closed in pleasure, the beat of the music coursing through my veins. Soon, warm hands were placed on each side of my waist. A feverish body, close to mine, kept time with the circular motion of my hips. I didn't need to open my eyes to know it was Tony. His familiar cologne snared my senses, encasing me in his large, hard body. I couldn't help myself and melted into him.

CHAPTER THIRTEEN

I couldn't take it anymore. I sat in my chair watching those luscious hips of Remi's sway back and forth like a medallion hypnotizing me. I loved the way she moved. And I wasn't the only man peeking at that voluptuous ass. There were several in our vicinity who were monitoring her. The fact that she was with me was irrelevant. My dick was pushing at the zipper of my jeans. I was sure I'd have an indentation if it wasn't released soon from its confines. I launched myself from my seat and made my way to the dance floor, to Remi.

My hands felt *right* holding her hips tight. My body sheathed in her heat. My dick hard as a rock from the way her ass was grinding against it. "I love watching you dance," I admitted, whispering in her ear. It was the truth. Her dancing was exactly what started this fucking infatuation with her. "I remember the first time I saw you dance. You captivated me. The only way to describe the effect you had on me. I couldn't keep my eyes off you the whole night," I informed her.

"You watched me?"

"I did. You didn't even know I was there, but you captured me that night. And you haven't let me go."

I didn't know if telling her I'd been watching her that night at the bar was wise or not. But right now, I didn't give a damn. I twisted her around to face me. Wanting her lips on mine immediately. I took her lips and crushed them to mine. They were so soft when I traced the seam with my tongue, asking for permission to enter. Remi readily opened up to me, and our tongues danced with one another just like our bodies. I deepened the kiss, holding her body close to mine. My hands roamed up and down her back and moved to cup that big ass. The maneuver ground her pussy against my erection. We both moaned at the sensation.

I moved my kisses to her cheek, down her neck and then up to her ear, capturing her lobe between my teeth, giving it a slight nibble. I whispered, "You ready to get out of here?"

Her nod was a relief, as I was hoping like hell she was as horny as I was. As soon as I saw the car up ahead of us, I pulled her in its direction. We were both running, laughing, and out of breath by the time the driver opened Remi's door. I ran around the back of the car, waving the driver off, when he scurried to open my door, reacting to my haste. I practically jumped in beside Remi, ready to sink into her, when I noticed her expression. She had her cell phone in her hand, flipping through her messages. I told the driver to take us back to the hotel, as I made sure the partition was up before we talked about what was happening.

"Remi, what's the matter? Is everything okay?" I reached for the mini fridge attached to the bar and poured both of us tumblers of whiskey. Remi readily downed hers.

"Thank you." She handed the glass back to me, and I poured her another. "Nothing, Erica is blowing up my phone. I promised her I would call, and I haven't yet." I wondered for a moment if she was telling me the truth. She didn't seem upset. If it was that asshole I'd talked to earlier, I think she would. *Bastard.*

Why though? Who would give up on a woman like Remi? I was just mad it took me this long to realize what a catch she was. It didn't matter to me whether or not she worked for me. I wanted her with me, and that was it. I didn't push her any further. We leave on Sunday, which meant I had a few more days to show her how it would be if she gave me a chance and eased my obsession.

The ride back was quick. The attraction between us was a slow simmer as we pulled up to the hotel. I fought with myself the entire ride over touching her, because if I did, I was sure I would fuck her in my car. And I didn't want that to be our first time together. My woman deserved better than a romp in the backseat. However, once I did, the fire we had while dancing rekindled and flared as if it was being fed an accelerant. I'd never had a woman who captured and kept my attention like Remi had. I'd dated models, celebrities, women as rich as I was, and none of them compared to Remi.

We stumbled our way to the private elevator. It took two times to maneuver the key card correctly so the scanner could read it. As soon as the doors closed, I pushed her against the wall, lavishing her with kisses. The black tank I chose for her showed just enough skin for me to wonder what was underneath. I kissed my way down from her neck to the swell of her chest. Moved to the left one, licked, and then moved to the right one. I gave each a small suck as Remi's moan echoed through the elevator. I wanted to feel them in my hands, see how soft and luscious they were. Squeezing both of her breasts as my lips crushed hers. Her nipples beaded beneath my palms as I ran my thumbs across them, causing her to arch into my touch.

"Ahhh," she moaned, the sensitivity getting the best of her. "Fuck me, please?" She pleaded as the *ding* of the elevator indicated we'd reached our destination.

I reluctantly backed away from her as the doors opened. My hand reached out to her, ecstatic when she readily put hers in mine so I could heave her through the doors. We laughed, stumbling through and over the threshold. The alcohol we had been drinking all day started to get to us. I'd waited so long to have this woman in my bed that my dick was jumping for joy. I hope she was ready for this because once I fucked her, there would be no turning back. She was mine.

CHAPTER FOURTEEN

"Is this really what you want?" he inquired as he led me over to the couch where I straddled his lap. I swear, I'd never thought I'd be in this situation, but I couldn't stop the avalanche that was sure to bury me from coming if I wanted to. For the better part of almost four years, this man staring up at me right now had given me nothing but grief. Today, he showed me this other side of himself, and if I wasn't careful, I would definitely lose my heart to him and get hurt. I wasn't ready for any of this, but right now, I didn't give a fuck. My head moved up and down to his question. It was all I could manage, throwing caution to the wind. Ready or not, and all that stuff. I may never get this opportunity again, and I didn't trust my voice for fear I would fuck up and say no.

His kisses distracted me from my overactive mind. All the *what-ifs* left as that wonderful tongue of his worked in and out of my mouth. I was so wrapped up in his kisses, I didn't even notice we'd made our way to the bedroom. His muscles bulged under his shirt as he gently placed me on my feet while he sat on the bed.

Tony crooked his finger, beckoning me to come. As I approached him, his hand shot up, halting me in the process.

"Stop," he ordered. "Strip."

A shiver ran through my body as I obeyed. I'd never turned to putty at a man's commanding voice, but Tony's just did something to my body I couldn't control. I readily toed off my sneakers, kicking them to the side and out of the way. I struggled to get my jeans undone. My hands wouldn't work. My palms were sweaty, and they trembled. I mean, I was about to sleep with my boss.

The realization almost caused me to falter.

Almost.

I took a deep breath to calm myself, but my hands still shook as I continued to do what he asked me. Finally, I stepped out of them as quickly as I could, but the glare Tony pierced me with had me stopping in my tracks. My breath hitched as I waited for what was next.

"Slowly," he commanded.

I agreed, standing there in my tank and panties, eager to do his bidding but, at the same time, unsure of how he saw me.

Was he pleased? Was I what he envisioned?

My position before him made me want to hide myself from his perusal, but the hunger I saw in his eyes, when I finally got the courage to raise my gaze to him, was like before that day in his office. Gah, that seemed such a long time ago. It made me refrain from concealing myself. I was vulnerable to him. The lustfulness in his eyes was unlike that of Mark's. I relished it. I wanted him to always have that look in his eyes for me.

"Now, the tank." I pulled it off quickly, forgetting his aforementioned directive to undress slowly. "Bra and panties," he grumbled.

My pussy fluttered at the demand in his voice. I was so damned eager to be with this man that I was sure I would never be the same after this experience.

I reached behind me, undid the hooks, and let my bra slide down my shoulders and arms leisurely before it fell to the floor. I reminded myself to slow down. It had become my mantra. Only to please him. He wanted to watch. The thought had my face heating with embarrassment. But I pushed through, remembering that look in his eyes. The softness of my panties glided down my legs, joining the rest of my clothes at my feet. I stepped out of them, waiting for my next command.

Exposed.

That was how I felt, but his reaction gave me confidence that being exposed to him was okay. Tony's piercing gaze burned straight to my soul. He stood and closed the distance between us, but he didn't touch me. My striptease had my body aching for his caress. I could feel the wetness pooling between my thighs in anticipation of what he had in store for me. When he finally made contact with my skin, it was almost more than I could endure. My eyes fluttered and closed, reveling in the feel of his hands trailing down my cheek to wrap around the back of my neck. The sensations sent shivers down my body as I leaned closer, trying to relieve some of the pressure within me. His hand entangled in my curls. A slight tug back exposed my neck. I winced at the pain and pressure, but it was soon forgotten the moment his lips touched the sensitive spot where my neck and shoulder met.

CHAPTER FIFTEEN

I should've stopped her. She drank way too much, and so did I. She was so beautiful to me, so carefree. It was an honor and privilege to put the desire and twinkle in her eyes. She was everything to me. She irrevocably had my heart. I think I was falling in love with her. She settled onto my lap, straddling me. Her confidence coming from the amount of alcohol we drank on our date at Riverwalk today, I was sure. I'd jacked off every night since we'd been here, constantly thinking about her. I relished her in my arms.

Once we made it to the bedroom and Remi stripped for me, the tight rein I had on myself let loose. I left a trail of heat making my way to the top of her breast. Remi's breathing was almost uncontrolled, and I was right with her. The surrounding air was thick and heavy, making it hard to breathe. Her nipples hardened under my scrutiny. She was on edge, nervous, like she'd always been with me. She trembled in my arms. But this time, it was for a different reason. She was so goddamned turned on. I didn't try to calm her fears. To me, it only heightened the experience. Her not knowing my next move was heady to me. She tried to wrap her arms around my neck. I pushed them away instead. Tasting one nipple, I applied a small suck, then nip. A moan escaped her and nearly brought me to my fucking knees. I'd longed to hear this woman in ecstasy. I switched to the other nipple, giving it the same treatment as the first.

Pleasure ran through me as her hips searched for my erection. My hands trailed up Remi's sides, caressing her curves. Her thickness excited me, and I squeezed the handful I'd found myself holding on to. Traveling back up to her breast, I took a minute to enjoy the weight of them as they spilled over my enormous hands. A long time ago, I realized she had a body on her, despite the conservative, frumpy clothes she wore to work to hide it, but I'd never expected it to be like this.

"You're so damn perfect," I whispered in between my ministrations.

With another nip, her hips rocked, finding my dick. I couldn't wait until I was inside her. She frantically reached for my belt buckle as my fingers brushed against her velvet heat. She was so fucking wet. Slipping my finger inside, I tested her tightness. I need to get her ready for me. Remi pitched forward into my touch again, hungry for more.

"You like that, baby?" I hissed in her ear, then licked her earlobe.

Remi shivered from the warmth of my breath on her already super-heated skin. My second finger didn't seem to be enough to dampen the fire I'd ignited in her, but I continued my ministrations as she mewled. She eventually got my pants unbuttoned and down, even with me eliciting groans from her as she started to rock to the rhythm I set with my fingers. She was coming undone, just the way I wanted to see her.

Taking my fingers back, a groan of disappointment followed as I stepped away from her so I could toe my boots and jeans off.

Once those were out of the way, Remi grabbed the hem of my shirt and tugged it over my head. It was almost as if she was as eager to be skin-to-skin as I was, so I let her finish undressing me. I relinquished control to her just for this moment. What I had in store for Remi required me to have the reins.

CHAPTER SIXTEEN

I had wondered what it was like to be at the receiving end of this man's attention. I'd never forget the look of satisfaction on his face or the mischievous one in his eyes when I walked in on him fucking that woman almost four years ago. And now, here he was in all his tawny glory as I gazed upon the most stunning man I'd ever seen. I hesitated to touch him without his permission, remembering that nothing happened between us, nor were we moving forward without his say-so. As much as I wanted to jump him and rub my body against him, I waited. His head bowed once, giving me the permission I required, and I ran my fingers down his muscled chest and scraped my nails across his abs. Gah, this man's body was everything. His muscles twitched under my attention, and his breath hitched.

His boxer briefs could barely contain his thick cock. My hands trembled with anticipation as I made my way to his waistband, pulling him free. Stroking him, wondering, not for the first time, how he would feel in my mouth. Our eyes met. The permission I sought was given. I knelt on the floor, stroking him from base to tip. A clear bead gathered at the head. I licked it, relishing it. The tang danced on my tongue and left me wanting more. From tip to base, my tongue laved his shaft lovingly, then I sucked the head into my mouth. My eyes, heavy with lust, closed in bliss as a savored him sliding in and out of my wet mouth. He gathered my curls in his hands, pumping in and out of my mouth. I hollowed my cheeks, tightening my grip on his dick as his pace quickened. Slowly pulling back to regain control from him, I used my hand to keep up with his pace. As I took him in, I opened my mouth wide, relaxing my throat, allowing him deeper into my mouth, before I swallowed, tightening my throat around his girth. He moaned, ripping himself from me.

"I don't want to come in your mouth," he snarled.

The sound of him losing his control caused my pussy to gush. I could feel my essence flowing down my thighs, and his absence from my mouth was palpable. Reaching for my prize once more, I tried to bring him back into my mouth only to be yanked to my feet with such force I almost fell forward. Tony's arms wrapped around me to steady me once more. He walked me backward to the far wall. With my back plastered against it, he once again devoured my mouth. His kisses turned my insides into liquid.

Suddenly, I was twisted around to face the wall. He pushed my right cheek against the cool wall. My bare breasts crushed against it. The friction against them felt so damn good, causing my arousal to heighten as Tony entered me, without warning, in one hard thrust. The suddenness of it stole my breath away. I could scarcely breathe, trying to adjust to the feeling of fullness. He pulled all the way out, then thrust back in again, harder this time, causing my feet to leave the floor. I was too helpless to do anything other than moan and claw for purchase on the wall. There was so much pleasure, it was painful.

"More," I begged.

Using a handful of my curls, he tipped my head toward his, crushing our lips together. The position would've been awkward if he wasn't ramming in and out of my pussy. The sensation of his body against mine only served to build more heat between us as the ecstasy rose, filling the room.

"This is fucking it, Remi. There's no going back now that I've tasted your sweet body," he growled in my ear. *Thrust in. Thrust out.* "You'll never wanna fuck anyone else when I'm finished with you." *Thrust in. Thrust out.* His strokes were getting harder, and I was on my way to the strongest, longest, orgasm I'd ever had in my life. "YOU. ARE. MINE." He punctuated every word with a thrust, causing my pussy to spasm around him. All I could do was agree with him as he continued to pump in and out of me, prolonging my orgasm until he fell over the edge himself.

He stayed with me, riding out the wave, until we were both too exhausted to stand any longer. His forehead rested on my back as we both tried to catch our breath. All of a sudden, I felt myself being swept up, carried to the bed. When the bed dipped, the soft caress of his lips touched my forehead as his arms wrapped around my waist. With the warmth covering my back, sleep took both of us away as the world and everyone in it faded to black.

When I woke, Tony was no longer beside me. The aroma of bacon and eggs with some of the strongest coffee on Earth had me rolling out of bed. A delicious soreness between my legs greeted me. He had awakened me several times during the night, bringing me to climax over and over again. There was a point where I didn't think I'd be able to take anymore, then he would ease off, staving my orgasm only to make me cum even harder. Damn, I had experienced nothing like that in my life. It was amazing.

"Good morning." I smiled as he entered the room with a tray filled with breakfast. I glanced at the clock on the side table. "Do we have time for all this?"

I sat up in bed so he could settle the tray over my lap. "Of course, we do. Eat up," he demanded.

The bacon was crispy thin, just like I liked it, and the eggs were fluffy like butter. I moaned, "This is so good."

"Glad you like it. I had the chef you hired come in this morning and make this for you," he explained. "I have to get my money's worth." The chuckle and smile he let off had me smiling as I took another bite of bacon.

"You eat up," he said, "and I'll go clean up the kitchen." He left me to my food. Watching him leave, I couldn't help but smile. I'd been doing that a lot since we'd been here.

I finished my breakfast and moved the tray to the bedside table so I could get up. I made my way to the restroom, eager to see if I looked any different in the mirror. Never had I been loved and cherished as much as I had been last night. I was beginning to think I had Tony all wrong. I'd seen a different side of him since we'd been here. Oh, he was still a ruthless businessman, hard-nosed, and didn't take any shit, as I saw firsthand in the meeting on Tuesday. If I hadn't squeezed his thigh, he would've told Mr. Smith to go fuck himself a few times.

I hopped into the shower as quickly as I could. He let me sleep too long. We had a meeting with the lawyers this morning. As far as I could tell, I had about an hour to get ready. Rummaging through the clothes he purchased for me. I was floored to see they were all designer. Tags with Armani, Gucci, and every other designer name I could think of, hung neatly in the massive walk-in closet.

"Wear the white Armani." His baritone echoed around the room, landing right between my legs. My pussy was instantly a faucet. I inhaled, then exhaled, trying to keep my composure. I pulled out the white, yes *white*, Armani suit he suggested. I didn't even want to see the price tag. "Put the royal blue silk tank on," he commanded.

"Oh, you're telling me how the dress now?" I said playfully, but I did as he asked, taking both to the bed.

He followed behind me with the same-colored heels from the closet. "Well, actually, I like you just like this." His voice an octave lower than normal. "Naked." If I glanced at him, I knew his eyes would mirror mine. His hand traced the bare skin on my back, sending tremors through my body. I had yet to figure out how this man could elicit such a response from me with only a touch. "But unfortunately, we don't have time for all the things I want to do to you, plus you're probably sore."

I sighed, "I have to admit, I am pretty sore."

I pulled on a panty and bra set he'd purchased. He held the tank out to me. Snatching it from him, I pulled it over my head. He was silent, which was totally opposite from how he had been these past few days we'd been together. Sitting on the bed, I pulled on the suit pants. His visage was so sad and regretful, I almost wished I hadn't said anything about being sore.

"I'm sorry," he said sheepishly. "It's just that I've wanted you for so damn long."

His confession blew me away. I had no idea he felt that way. I mean, he was my boss, for God's sake. A fact I tried not to dwell on.

Buttoning my pants, I tried reassuring him. "It's fine. Really. I'm fine. Don't worry."

I made my way to the vanity to do something to the rat's nest on top of my head. At night, I usually put it up, but with all the lovemaking we were doing last night, I didn't get a chance. Plus, he liked to be able to put hands through my hair when we were having sex. I styled it up into a high ponytail, wrapping it around my fingers so tendrils hung on each side. Light makeup and a nude gloss were the finishing touches.

The entire time, he'd been sitting on the bed watching me. Not so long ago, his stare made me uncomfortable; now, it set my soul on fire. "I'm almost ready," I announced, brushing my hair up one last time to make sure it wasn't frizzy.

"Not quite," he stated, crossing over to me, putting something around my neck, then stepping back.

Gasping, my hand went straight to the pendant hanging just above my cleavage. It was one of the most exquisite pieces of jewelry I'd ever seen. It was a small silver chain with a diamond-encrusted, heart-shaped key hanging from it. I understood the analogy, key-to-my-heart.

"It's platinum," he announced, with a Cheshire Cat grin across his face. "I had it made for you when we got here."

"I can't accept this." I reached around my neck to unhook it.

His hand tightened on the back of my neck, halting my action. "I had it made for you, so it's yours," he rumbled. "Wear it today and the earrings I bought as well."

He walked out of the room without further debate of the matter. I sighed because somehow, I'd hurt his feelings. I wasn't sure what to do about it. The Tony St. Clair I'd known for four years was not the same man I'd been spending time with. But for some reason, my head couldn't reconcile the two. My eyes flashed to the mirror, admiring the lovely necklace. Tony had great taste.

"We have to go," he bellowed from the living room of the suite.

Sliding my feet into my shoes, I pulled on my suit jacket. Before I could grab my bag, he was already in the elevator waiting on me. Regardless of how I felt about the jewelry, I wore it anyway, partly to appease him and partly because there was no time to take it off before he made his demand for us to leave.

The elevator ride down was silent. Trying to restrain from rolling my eyes, I sighed during the entire car ride to Transient because of his annoying attitude. It was really starting to piss me off. I pulled out my laptop to finish the few notes he didn't allow me to finish yesterday before our lunch. By the time we pulled up to Transient, the notes were done, and I'd emailed them out to all parties involved in this contract, including the lawyers.

The man sitting beside me on our way back to our hotel room was ruthless, and that was the understatement of the year. We understood going in that Steve Smith was a merciless businessman. He made his billions by undermining people, backstabbing them, making deals behind allies and competitors' backs alike, but he'd fucked with the wrong one when he tried to take on Tony St. Clair.

The meeting was tense, with an underlying atmosphere of violence. My eyes stayed wide, as my head swiveled back and forth between the two men and their lawyers. Mr. Smith tried to hold out for more money when they had an ironclad deal. But the agreed upon price was there in black and white. Mr. Smith's lawyer picked up the contract I provided for him and read. We gave him a few minutes to read it in its entirety. Then he leaned over to Mr. Smith and whispered in his ear. I was sure he was letting Mr. Smith know the agreement was solid, and in the end, Mr. St. Clair got what he wanted, and Mr. Smith got his money. On the ride back, the silent treatment continued. I couldn't take it anymore. I turned to address him when my cell phone blared through the quiet. The fear of the person on the other line being Mark caused me to hesitate.

"Hello."

Hopefully, my rude tone would deter him.

"Well, fuck you too, bitch." A chuckle followed, and I immediately cracked a smile. "Why ain't you called me, chic?" Erica asked.

Erica always had a knack for knowing when I needed a laugh. With Tony not talking to me, I really needed it.

"Girl, hush." I giggled. Glancing out the corner of my eye, I could see Tony physically relax, and I wondered why he was uptight over my phone call. He pulled his own phone out, scrolled and started to type. My attention was drawn back to Erica. "I've just been busy," I said around snickers. My eye cut back to Tony, and his smirk gave me hope he wouldn't give me the silent treatment the rest of our trip.

"I *bet*! So, what *have* you done with Mr. *Fine Ass* St. Clair?" I never thought I'd appreciate the melanin in my skin the way I did right now, no one could see me blush as I thought about all we did last night and into the early morning. I played with the charm on the necklace he gave me, as I decided exactly what to tell her. "Come on, sis! Give me the detes," she whined.

Damn glad I didn't have her on speaker. I was mortified enough as it was. If she even got a whiff of what I'd been doing with our boss, I didn't know what would happen. "We're in the car on our way back from a meeting. What's been up with you?" I asked, changing the subject on the sly. Or at least I *thought* I was sly.

A tsk came over the line, and I grinned. She knew me so fucking well. "Uh, uh. Don't try to change the subject. Tell *me*."

It was safe to tell her about lunch, I decided she was gonna see it anyway from the pictures people were snapping of us. "Erica, this has been the best time of my life," I gushed, knowing Tony was listening. "We went to this expensive restaurant. I couldn't even pronounce the name. And then we took a walk on the Magnificent Mile," I added.

Erica interrupted. "Oh, did you go shopping?"

I laughed. "No, but he bought me a closet full of clothes. We went dancing. It was *so* incredible." Once I divulged, I held my phone away from my ear because the squeal was coming. I kept a countdown in my head. Tony looked over at me with his eyebrows scrunched. Then Erica's high-pitched scream was so loud it echoed through the car, and Tony's confusion turned to surprise. The look on his face had me peeling with laughter.

We made our way up to the hotel as Erica and I said our

goodbyes. "Erica, I'll talk to you later, we just pulled up to the hotel. I'll text you." I did have a lot to tell her. All this shit with Mark was driving me crazy. I needed to tell somebody. Even though he was on my mind, my smile was still present when we entered the elevator. Like before, Tony's hand cradled my lower back, escorting me into the elevator. As soon as the doors closed, he kissed me. No matter how awkward today had been, I couldn't swallow the moan bubbling up from deep down. The sound encouraged him to deepen our kiss. He pulled away from me and touched his forehead to mine. Both of our breaths came out as pants.

"I'm so fucking sorry. I've been an asshole today," he declared.

And I didn't correct him because he was, but I did apologize to him for so readily throwing his gift away. "And I apologize for being inconsiderate and ungrateful. It really is a beautiful gift." My hand landed on the charm laying against my chest.

"I think we need to talk," he announced as the elevator doors opened. He led me out and directly to the couch. The warmth from his hand seeped into my skin and made a trail down to my lady parts. I laid my bag at my feet and settled in next to him. I couldn't help how my heart raced. This talk we were about to have seemed heavy. I realized...*I was scared.* "Remi, I know this,"—he pointed between the two of us—"is unconventional."

I snorted, "Unconventional? You're my boss. We are not even gonna talk about how shitty you've been to me all these years."

At least he had the decency to look guilty about it.

He rubbed his hand down his face, rubbing that full beard I loved to feel scrub against my chin as he kissed me and tickled my privates when he went down on me. "I know. I know, and I'm sorry. But Remi, I need to tell you." He paused, seeming to collect his thoughts. "I'm not coming out of this week thinking this is just some fling. I want this. I want us," he admitted.

I was speechless and clueless, unclear of what was happening here. "You don't have to say anything. You don't even have to decide right now. I just want you to be aware. I've known I wanted you for months now." He grabbed my hands, bringing them to his lap. "I have two confessions to make."

He was rambling. I was speechless because normally he was so polished. He was a rock. Unshakable. But right now, I saw a man who lacked confidence and fidgeted in anticipation of my reaction.

Fuck, this was gonna be bad.

I took a deep breath and tried to refrain from passing judgment until I heard what he had to say to me.

"Well, just tell me. You're killing me and scaring me to be honest."

He squeezed my hands tighter and blew out a breath. I'd never seen him this vulnerable. He was supposed to be impenetrable. "I answered your phone while you were in the shower yesterday." My eyes widened at his confession, but I remained silent only squeezing his hand, encouraging him to continue. I needed to see where he was going with this. "It was a man on the line." My body deflated because he knew about Mark. My eyes lowered to my lap, and I focused on our clasped hands. My explanation didn't come right away, so he pushed on. "I didn't get his name, but I figured he was the person who upset you yesterday. I wanted to see who made you so downtrodden. You were having such a good time, and I was upset because they took that from you."

"So, what happened?" Afraid that somehow Mark had ruined everything for me, I had to ask.

"Nothing," he announced. "Well, that's not true," he backtracked. "I told him I was your boyfriend. He hung up after that." Well, that would explain why I hadn't gotten any more calls from him since yesterday. "I hate to ask, Remi, but I need to know what happened."

This I definitely didn't want to talk about. It was obvious if

Mark was going to be calling, and Tony had noticed how upset it made me, I had to tell him. So, I spilled everything. I blew out the pent-up breath I was holding, dreading what I was about to divulge.

"At the start, Mark was great. My dad loved him. He came from an excellent family. Treated me like he cherished the ground I walked on." I sighed because those were wonderful times. "I never thought he would cheat. We were at this club, having the time of our lives, when this woman walked up to us. She was pissed because Mark was out with me." I took a minute to gather my thoughts. "She started yelling about him cheating on her and questioning how he could do that to her. Shit! How could he do that to *me*? We were living together."

"So, what did he do? What did you say?"

"He dragged me out of that club so fast, I didn't know what was going on. We drove straight home. It didn't hit me until he actually started to defend himself. Saying he didn't know her. He only loves me. You know. The usual stuff men say when we catch them cheating." I regretted it the moment the statement came flying out of my mouth.

"No, I don't." It was so nonchalant that I couldn't help but believe him.

My apologies rushed out, but he waved them away, so I continued. "Anyway, for whatever reason, I *wanted* to believe him. I guess I thought I could change him?" I rose from the couch, making my way to the window and stared out at the river making its way past us without a care in the world. He hovered without touching me.

He encouraged me to continue my story. "So, you took him back?"

"Yep, I took him back. And it was like nothing had ever happened. It was back to normal for about two months. Afterward, it went to shit," I admitted. "I was in a restaurant with an old friend I'd lost touch with since college and had bumped into, when two women approached us."

"Damn," he whispered, rubbing my shoulder to comfort me.

Turning my head up to him, I grinned. His touch was reassuring.

"Exactly. They asked if they could sit. My friend agreed, and then these two women proceeded to tell me how both of them had been in a relationship with Mark for over a year. A fucking year! I couldn't believe it." He ran his hand down my back as we continued to stare out at the river. There was no judgment, and it was soothing. "After that meeting, I went straight home, called my dad and told him I found a job in New York that started the next day. I packed my shit and went to my dad's house to see if he would go with me. He declined, so we said our goodbyes, and I never looked back." I sighed when I finished.

He gathered me into his arms and gave me a gentle squeeze. "I'm so sorry that happened to you."

"I was humiliated. It was like everyone had information about my relationship except me. I don't know how they knew who I was or even how they found one another. I didn't ask. After that, I believed I was inadequate. I wasn't worthy." I couldn't hold back the tears. They weren't all out sobs as they once had been, but it still hurt to learn I wasn't enough for the person I thought loved me unconditionally. "I hadn't talked to him since I packed up and left. I even changed my number when I moved to the city."

After finishing, I felt as if a weight had been lifted from my shoulders. Erica was the only other person who knew why I left, not even my father knew the total truth.

"So, why is he calling now? After all this time?" he questioned.

"Honestly, that's what I'd like to find out."

CHAPTER SEVENTEEN

Basically, what I was hearing was that Remi's asshole ex-boyfriend cheated on her, and now she had absolutely no faith in men. That made me feel even worse about how I treated her all those years and recently as well. I apologized to her again. "I'm sorry I acted the way I did all these years. I didn't want to believe I wanted you so badly. It's why I acted like such a jerk."

"Don't worry about it," she waved it off. "I should apologize to you. Like I said, it was insensitive of me. The gift was very thoughtful. Thanks."

I didn't get my hopes up too much, though. I still needed to tell her about the cancellation, but what she shared with me shifted the atmosphere in the room. She should be happy and carefree like she was when she spoke with Erica. So, I decided not to tell her about it just yet. This week was about her. Wining and dining Remi, giving her a glimpse of how it would be between us if she agreed to this relationship, was my plan.

"Go get dressed and wear comfortable shoes."

She chuckled when I hauled her to her feet. "Another surprise date? You're trying to spoil me. I'm going to miss this when we get back to reality," her singsong voice rang out as she made her way into the bedroom.

I didn't say anything about her comment. She knew how I felt. What I expected. Apparently, she didn't believe me. Hopefully, what I planned for her today and tonight would help her change her mind. I texted Sean again. Sean was a friend from college I'd kept in touch with over the years. He was a tech guy like me, but he could get just about any information you wanted. He was also a private investigator. The information Remi gave me was a tremendous help. I had texted him while she was on the phone with Erica and asked him to run the number I had memorized of the guy—Mark, she said his name was—who was calling her.

ME

No need for the search I texted you about earlier. I know who's been calling her.

SEAN

Ok, good. I was just about to call my contact.

ME

Thanks. Like I said, don't worry about it. If I need anything else, I'll let you know.

SEAN

Okay, anytime.

We changed out of our tailored suits and put on something a little more comfortable. I planned to take her to the aquarium. Chi-Town was one of those cities you couldn't help but love. I'd been here a few times and had gotten the chance—although not that often—to go to some of these places I'd experienced with her. I was in awe of all the beautiful and amazing places, but I wanted Remi to have those experiences too.

Remi having the best time possible at the aquarium was all I cared about. I was confident Remi would love the private tour. At first, the manager was against it, but the amount of money I gave her was what they'd make in a single day. Also, pledging a healthy forthcoming donation helped sway her decision.

The ride over was brief. Along the way, we answered texts and checked emails. Even though I was on a romantic getaway to win the girl of my dreams, I still had a company to run. The joy on Remi's face was worth it when we arrived in front of the aquarium. It was like her entire face glowed, and her smile nearly brought me to my knees. The manager met us at the door and introduced us to our guide. The tour included all the animal exhibitions, and I booked their events venue so we could have a private dinner for just the two of us.

We made our way through each exhibit. More than once, Remi clapped and bounced on the balls of her feet in excitement. My heart swelled seeing her reaction. It was then I realized, for sure, that I was in love with her. She was it for me, and I'd do whatever it took to make her happy and love me, too.

We made our way to the event venue. My eyes trained on Remi. I wanted to make sure I didn't miss a single gasp, twinkle of her eye, or smile when the door opened, revealing the exquisite room.

Tables covered in white linens, with six Plexiglas chairs to each, were lined up on either side of the center walkway. Each table was set with water glasses and flatware and decorated with a raised dais in the center, no thicker than an inch, holding three clear glass vases surrounded by lit votive candles and with pink, yellow, and orange petals scattered around them. The largest centerpiece was adorned with vases of emerging banana leaves, while the two smaller vases on either side were filled with water and lit votive candles.

"Oh wow! This is so beautiful," she whispered, and I couldn't help but smile.

"It is, but let's move on."

She allowed me to usher her down the aisle through an archway. In front of us, in the center of the room, was a floor-to-ceiling round aquarium full of tropical fish and coral, as if it were holding up the ceiling. Although the room could house several hundred people, there was only a single intricately decorated round table with two chairs settled in front of the aquarium.

The white linen-covered table was set with water glasses and flatware. The elaborate centerpiece consisted of two martini glasses about a foot high flanking a bigger bowl-shaped, blue-lit vase, the same hue as the water. About a foot high, the vase was full of stemless roses shaped into a ball and included two kinds of yellow flowers I didn't recognize scattered within. The base was lit up with a blue light, mimicking the hue of the aquarium.

Her arms flew around me, and she sniffled as she buried her face into my chest. "You did all this for me?"

It came out muffled as she tried to hide her tears. I pulled her away from me to gaze into her eyes. With my thumb, I wiped the tears slowly, tracing them down her cheeks.

"Hey, don't cry," I whispered. "I thought this would make you happy."

I continued to wipe her tears until they slowed. When she regained her composure, she reassured me, "These are happy tears. I've never had anyone do something like this before just for me."

"I'm happy I'm giving you a lot of your firsts," I admitted, kissing her on the forehead and leading her to our table.

As we settled in, the room filled with soft, mellow jazz, played by a band in the room's corner. Although jazz nights were usually on Wednesdays, I'd convinced the manager to make an exception. Remi seemed to love all types of music, from what I could tell, so I couldn't let her have this experience without music.

Once again, we had agreed to leave our phones in the car. I didn't want that fucker Mark ruining our time together. She also agreed not to answer his calls or texts without me around. If she did, it was to be on speaker so I could hear. However, he hadn't called her again since I answered yesterday.

Soon, our meals came out of the kitchen, and we ate in companionable silence. I enjoyed the way she savored her food and how she exclaimed when she discovered something new while watching the different fish swim by. But dessert was her favorite course. Every time she put the sweetness in her mouth, her eyes shut and the moan she released went straight to my dick. "Remi," I warned. The innocence in her eyes told me she had no idea what she was doing to me, but I was sure she saw my desire. Hers turned from purity to mirroring my own. "Are you ready to leave?" I inquired, because I was.

I was ready to dive into her sweet pussy with my tongue. Remi was particularly vocal when my tongue was deep within her. I loved to hear the sounds she made.

"Yes." Her answer was deep and throaty. The combination, sexy as hell.

I'd planned a walk through the botanical gardens, but if I didn't have her now, I wouldn't be able to focus on our walk. Pretty sure, I would've just been thinking about burying myself in her balls deep or trying to find a place in the garden to do so.

I gathered her from her chair. We all but sped walk out of the building. By the time we reached the car, I barely had time to get the partition up before she had my dick out of my jeans. Her hands on me were like a dream, and my cock danced in anticipation of her touch. She engulfed me to my base and then slowly rose up off it until there was a pop as she released from her mouth. She licked me from base to tip before she covered the head, engulfing me again. The sensation of her tongue caressing me had my mind blown. I could feel my eyes rolling into the back of my head. And then she gave a gentle suck. "Ahhhh..." I moaned and grabbed the back of her head.

The need for my fingers to intertwine in her curls was uncontrollable. I removed every bobby pin I could find and wrapped her hair around my fist as my cock repeatedly hit the back of her throat. The warm sensation of her mouth was gratifying. Despite the tight grip on her hair, Remi managed to pull back almost letting my dick fall out of her mouth, then closing her lips around me, taking me back into the confines of heat. My balls tightened as her attention on me came faster while I pumped into her mouth, matching the rhythm she set.

"Remi, oh…you feel so good. That mouth. Damn baby, so *good*," I declared, continuing to pump in and out. *In and out.* "Baby, I don't wanna come this way," I pleaded.

Her head game was that good. I'd never begged a woman for *anything* before. If I had to beg for the pussy, it wasn't worth my time. But for Remi, I would crawl on my fucking hands and knees to get that. She had me right where she wanted me. I preferred coming in her sweet pussy, so I tried to take my dick out of her mouth, but instead Remi's lips wrapped tighter around my dick. Her hands clamped around my thighs, restricting my mobility. Restrained. She sucked harder, and I felt as if my soul was being sucked from my body. I couldn't help it. "Shit," I groaned again, praising her for her skills.

Pumping into her mouth, *once. Twice.* Her cheeks hollowed, and she gave my dick one last hard suck from the base to the tip, and I couldn't hold back my seed any longer. I used two hands to grab her head, tugging her forward, burying as much of my dick as she could take inside and down her throat until I was spent, and my cum dribbled from her mouth.

As I stared down into her face, I couldn't help but think about how much I loved her. Remi on her knees was a sight I wanted to see for the rest of my days. My breaths were coming hard, as if I'd just done my full workout routine. When I saw the tip of her pink tongue snake out to catch the dribble of cum escaping down her chin, my knees buckled. I was sure I'd fall if I were standing.

"You're killing me." I groaned when the sight had my dick coming back to life.

She giggled and tucked me back into my pants, then zipped me up before she settled in the seat beside me. I promised myself right then that I would treasure her body when we got back to the room. I didn't just get, I also gave.

CHAPTER EIGHTEEN

I couldn't believe I just did that. Tony was right. He had been there for a lot of my "firsts." I didn't know what I was going to do when we got back home. Maybe we'd go back to the way it had always been. There was no way we could maintain this…whatever *this* was between us. The thought saddened me as I realized that in three days this man had made me fall in love with him. Doubts and depression got pushed to the back of my mind. We still had a few more days left in Chicago, so I promised myself I was going to enjoy the moment and not worry about what happened when we got back to St. Clair Technologies.

His lips at my temple brought me out of the doom and gloom in my head. I welcomed the love as we arrived at the hotel. Tony opened the door, waving off the driver so he could help me out and into his arms. As we entered the lobby, a bombardment of flashes and questions from the media encompassed us.

"Mr. St. Clair, who is this on your arm?"

"Are the two of you a couple?"

He pushed me through the crowd toward the elevator.

"Mr. St. Clair, is it true you have a secret love child?"

My breath hitched at the question, but I tried not to show any reaction on my face. My glimpse at him didn't reveal the truth one way or another. Thankfully, the elevator doors opened before I could do anything stupid, like cry in front of all those people. Why wouldn't he tell me he had a child? If you're professing love and a relationship, as he had, why not mention anything about a family? Fuck, I had to get out of there. I couldn't do Mark all over again.

The ride up was silent. When he tried to hold my hand, I refused to let him touch me. I couldn't do this. My emotions were all over the place. I was miserable and on the brink of tears. Angry at myself for allowing hope to seep in and sad because I was already in love with him. Same song, different verse, I opened my heart and in return got secrets.

"Remi," he called. I didn't answer, just went straight to the room, slamming the door. I was afraid I'd fall for the bullshit, then it would be Mark all over again. Me being a fool and blind to what was right in front of my face. I sat on the bed, trying to get myself together. I mean, why *wouldn't* he have a child out there somewhere. I was introduced to the company by him fucking a woman on his desk! Rich, handsome, all kinds of women falling all over him, so of course, this was bound to happen.

"I have to get out of here," I mumbled, trying to take my mind off the sound of my heart shattering into a million pieces.

My mind was set. I grabbed my bag from the closet and pulled the clothes I brought off the racks and anything I owned from the dresser in the back of the closet. I threw everything in the bag quickly, pausing at the sound of his voice coming through the door before he barged in. His face almost crumpled when he spied my packed bag.

"Remi," he began, his eyes swimming with hurt and confusion, but then the emotions I saw there were gone within a split second, replaced by a poker face.

The stoic man I'd known for four years was back. His eyes no longer showed the tenderness they had for me these past few days. And even though it broke my heart to see the mirth fall away from his features, I couldn't be with another Mark. My heart couldn't take it, and I just didn't have the energy. I grabbed my phone from my back pocket, called a *Lyft*, and made my way to the elevator without him stopping me. I was conflicted because part of me wanted to hold on tight to him, to our budding romance, kicking and screaming, but the other part wanted to run away from him as fast as I could, away from the heartache. That was the part that won out. When the elevator opened, I was relieved because if I had to wait for it to ascend, I might have changed my mind.

Thankfully, there was no media in the lobby, and the tears I'd been holding back pushed through as soon as I slid into the back seat. "Take me to the airport," I squeezed through bated breath. *What the hell was I doing?* My mind whirled as I tried to get hold of exactly the things I needed to take care of. I needed to get home. I was used to making lists to get my work done, so my plan to get home was no different. *Guess I was anal like that, never noticed it before.* The thought seeped into my head, and a chuckle burst forth at the absurdity.

Mentally, I checked off everything I needed to do. First and foremost, I needed to purchase my ticket home. The *Lyft* pulled up to the drop off, reaching for my belongings, I realized I'd left my purse in the penthouse. I was *not* going back because if I did, I'd fold, just as I did with Mark. No repeating *that* mistake.

"Shit!" I shouted, not giving a fuck at this point who was watching, angry with myself for forgetting the one thing I absolutely need.

Then it dawned on me I'd also forgotten my computer, but it belonged to the company, so it was safe with my boss. I had to go back to seeing him as the man he was before this trip. My hopes were too high, thinking maybe, just *maybe*, we could make this work, but I saw now that there was always going to be controversy, always going to be drama, and always going to be our differences hovering between us. He was a billionaire, one of the most eligible bachelors in the world. And I was just his personal assistant. Thank God for my wallet app. Opening it, I paid the *Lyft* driver and then rushed to the counter to book the first flight back to New York. Luckily, there was one leaving within the next hour. It gave me time to check my bag and take a breath. My body and mind were exhausted from crying, and my heart was slowly hardening.

As soon as I found a spot to rest, I texted Erica.

ME

Hey, chica. I'm coming home. 😌 I'll be there later tonight.

Immediately, a *ding* sounded.

ERICA

Oh no. What happened, honey?

I blew out a sigh, willing myself not to cry in the middle of the airport, but he had ripped my soul from my body.

ME

It's a long story. Pick me up from the airport, and I'll tell you on the ride. Can I stay with you tonight?

ERICA

Of course, honey. I'll see you in two hours. <3

ME

Thank you so much, honey. I'll see you soon. <3

Turning off my phone and scooping up my bag, I headed to the terminal. Relief overwhelmed me as I finally left this nightmare behind. I wondered what to do about work. I couldn't afford to pick up and move again. Besides, I was tired of running from love. Granted, I never wanted to see Mr. St. Clair again, but I liked my job, it paid well, and I excelled at what I did. I'd be able to separate the two. I was sure of it, and if he couldn't, well then, that would just be tough. I focused on pushing all that to the back of my mind until my head was clear and my heart didn't work so much. My workweek didn't start until Monday. Maybe by then, I'd figure out what to do.

The moment I stepped off the plane and turned my phone back on, I was bombarded with a barrage of text messages. I traversed through the terminal and into the airport on the lookout for Erica. One was from her telling me she was waiting. Unfortunately, there were no messages from Tony…I mean, Mr. St. Clair.

The other dozen or so were from Mark. They were so crude I could barely get through any of them. Some asked how I could do this to him. Others were more aggressive, saying I must think I was fucking something for bagging a billionaire or just calling me a whore, slut, or bitch.

Rolling my eyes, I delete them in the process. Still not sure how the hell he got my number, but it was definitely something I needed to get to the bottom of. One thing was for sure. I was appreciative that Tony held him off, at least for a little while, although Mark was not his problem. He's mine.

"Oh, honey!" The sound drawled behind me.

Instantly, I cracked a smile when I turned to see Erica practically speed walking through the airport with her arms wide open, ready to engulf me. I met her halfway and welcomed her warmth as it seeped into my skin.

This thing with Tony was worse than when I found out Mark cheated, but why?

"Thanks for coming, sis," I sniffed as I pushed myself out of her arms.

We headed out of the terminal to her car. To her credit, she didn't ask me anything, even though she wanted to. Erica was nosy and a gossiper, so me not talking was killing her. The frown marring her face told me it was more than that. She was worried about me. But I just wanted to take this opportunity to relax and clear my thoughts before I decided to talk to her.

The ride back afforded me time to nap, and before I knew it, we pulled into her complex and headed inside. Unlike me, Erica lived on the first floor of her building, which I appreciated at this particular time. My body was weary, so tackling stairs wasn't what I wanted to do. We walked right through the gate and into the unguarded building. There were no security measures here like at my building. Her neighborhood wasn't a bad one. It was just that as a single woman, you could never be too careful. I told Erica all the time that it was dangerous. But more than once, she had turned her nose up at me for complaining about her building. And I was adamant about the fact that every neighbor knew and watched out for one another. She flung the door open, pulling her keys from the keyhole and grabbing my bag and hand. She threw it into the recliner in the corner, then led me to the couch before scurrying to the kitchen to warm up the coffee on the maker.

Her apartment was homey, the exact opposite of mine. She had a plush couch decorated with floral-printed pillows in its corners. A throw rug in the middle of the floor and more floral pillows tucked in the corners of the loveseat added a cozy touch. I snatched one pillow as if it was my last thread to life. Erica settled in next to me as she handed me a steaming hot cup of coffee.

"All right, spill," she demanded.

I couldn't help but snort. She absolutely hadn't grasped the concept of sympathy. Couldn't she see I was wallowing in my own pity? I took a sip of the coffee. "There's nothing to tell."

She gave me a skeptical look as one of her eyebrows was almost touching her hairline. "If there's nothing to tell, then do you care to explain why you and Mr. St. Clair are plastered all over *ET* and *TMZ*?"

I almost choked. "What are you talking about?"

She immediately pulled out her phone and launched *Twitter*. Finding the article she was referring to, she shoved her phone in my face. I took her phone and then read:

Is This Playboy Billionaire Finally Off the Market?

The headline was followed by several pictures of me and Mr. St. Clair kissing after he broke my fall getting out of the kayak. A picture of us in the bubble at the winery. One of us dancing and kissing *again.* I didn't want to see anymore and handed her back her phone, sighing, not because I was tired, but because I missed him.

My eyes swelled with tears, but I refused to let them fall. I sensed Erica hovering, not sure exactly what to do, then eventually her arms wrapped around me. "You love him, don't you?"

I didn't trust my voice. I was barely holding on, so I dipped my head at once and didn't try to hold the dam back anymore. A good fifteen-minute cry commenced before I was able to get myself together. I had other things to worry about, like what to do with Mark.

"There is so much I do need to tell you, though." I managed, finally feeling like talking to her.

She made her way to the kitchen, dumping the old coffee to

get another pot started, and I followed, planting myself at the bar.

Wrinkles between her eyes and a snarl on her lips, she pointed her finger directly at my chest. "I knew you were holding out on me. Spill."

My hands went up in surrender while trying to hold back my laughter. "Okay. Okay. Well, Mark has been calling me for one," I said, getting directly to the juice.

All pretense of her anger was gone, and she moved to sit beside me. "Oh my god! How the hell did he even get your number?"

I shook my head as I thought about that for a second. With all that had been happening with Mr. St. Clair, I hadn't had time to really think about it. "I have my suspicions, but I don't know."

Erica was the type who loved drama. If she didn't have any in her life, she was happy to wallow in yours.

Her eyes lit up, thriving on the bit of information I'd given her. "Well, who do you think it was?" I didn't say right away, and I almost hated to pull him into this mess. "Come on, Remi, don't leave me in suspense."

The way her eyes stretched wide was comical, and if it wasn't for the seriousness of the situation, I would've been laughing my ass off.

"Okay," I relented, sighing. "I think it was my father."

I'd never told my father the reason Mark and I had broken up because he'd always liked Mark, believing he was an exceptional man and the perfect man for his daughter. I didn't want to disappoint my father with my decision to leave Mark. I had so many other failed relationships. And Tony was just another one to add to the ever-growing list.

"I didn't tell him what happened between us. I'll call him tomorrow." I slid off the stool and headed to the coffeemaker to pour me another cup of coffee.

"You want a cup?" I asked, reaching for her mug.

I poured both of us a cup, inhaling the rich aroma of the coffee. I handed Erica hers so she could doctor it the way she liked, while I added plenty of creamer and sugar to mine. Once I was done, I told Erica about Tony answering my phone. "So, apparently, while I was in the shower, Mark called, and Mr. St. Clair answered my phone."

Laughter peeled out of her, and I couldn't do anything other than laugh right along with her. We laughed so hard, tears fell, and I got a stitch in my side. While struggling to catch my breath, I wiped away happy tears.

"Oh my god, I would've been seething mad," she declared once she was able to speak again.

"Right, and I thought I would be, too. But there was nothing said out of the way. He told him that he was my boyfriend. Mark didn't call again until I got off the plane. I assume he saw the articles same as you." Which led me to what happened. "In hindsight, I probably should've let him explain," reasoning aloud. "But honestly, I didn't think it would make a difference in whether or not I stayed with him because I had already made my mind up. I wasn't taking this any further than Chicago."

She stared at me like I had two heads. "Are you kidding me?"

Her scrutiny made me fidget and think that maybe I'd done the wrong thing. "Well..." I stammered. "I just thought it would be a fling."

"So, you just left and didn't even let him explain?" she squawked at me.

My fingers gravitated to the key-to-my-heart necklace Tony gave me, and I pulled the charm back and forth across the platinum chain. It caught Erica's attention, and she moved into my space to get a closer look at the necklace.

"Holy shit," she whispered, and locked eyes with me. "Are those real diamonds?"

I nodded, letting the charm go as she took it into her hand.

"Inlaid in platinum. It was a gift from Tony."

"Holy shit," she yelled again, letting go of the charm.

"I forgot I even had it on," I admitted, touching my fingers to the charm again.

"I can't believe he bought you a diamond and platinum necklace." Her voice was full of awe as she scrambled back to her seat and grabbed her mug. "You want a refill?" She questioned as she poured herself another cup. We had almost drunk the entire pot at this point. I handed her my cup and zoned out as she poured. I didn't even mention to her about the clothes and the other necklace and earrings set I left in the room. I would've left this one too, had I not forgotten about it. "And you didn't let him explain about the baby daddy thing?" She shook her head as she came back to the bar and handed me my coffee. "Damn, girl."

There was disappointment laced in her words. I didn't expect this reaction from her. "You're supposed to be on my side," I whined, savoring the coffee I sipped.

"I'm not taking sides, Remi." She gave me an understanding smile and covered my free hand with hers. "But you have to admit, just leaving the way you did was cold-hearted as hell."

I listened to her perspective because she was right. "I can't do this again, Erica. I can't trust him to take care of my heart. I did that once, and I'm paying for it as we speak."

My cell phone rang, cutting through my thoughtful silence. Ten o'clock was blaring in emerald green on Erica's stove. *Who in the world would call me at this time?* My heart raced as I secretly hoped it was Tony, but, of course, my hopes splintered as Mark's number flashed across my screen again. *Why do I even remember his number?*

"Answer it," Erica encouraged me, "it might be Mr. St. Clair."

I shook my head and roll my eyes. "It's Mark."

"Well, answer it anyway and cuss his ass out," she hyped.

A grin stretched across my face from ear to ear. No matter how down I was or the situation, she always found a way to put me at ease or make me laugh. With newfound courage and resolve, I answered his call.

"What do you want?" I groused out, sick of him harassing me.

"You."

I rolled my eyes. "Put him on speaker," Erica whispered.

I pressed the speaker button so she could hear his end of the conversation. He sounded like he was in a restaurant or bar because of the music and constant conversation in the background.

"Remi, do you understand me," he slurred.

My eyes caught Erica as she mouthed that Mark was drunk, causing me to bob my head in agreement.

"Yes, I heard you, but why are you calling me all of a sudden? Why won't you just leave me alone? I left you for a reason."

The line was silent, and I hoped he'd hung up. Unfortunately, I was wrong.

His voice took on a guttural quality I'd never witnessed before. "I'm not fucking good enough for you, Remi? Why? Because I don't have money like that motherfucker you've been letting hit that sweet pussy."

My stomach roiled in disgust. I couldn't listen to anything else he was saying. "Fuck you, Mark. You don't know shit about me or Tony, so shut your mouth!" I was seething. I wasn't gonna let him talk about Tony like that. "And if you don't stop harassing me, you'll have some problems."

When I hung up, Erica was doing a whole dance because of how I handled myself with Mark. To tell you the truth, there was a time I would've folded and went back to him. I stood up to him. My four years in New York had taught me how to be independent and be my own woman. It was the best move I'd ever made in my life.

We sat up for another hour and talked more about the business side of the trip. If we continued to talk about any of the experiences I shared with Tony, I would have cried myself to sleep. After we caught up, we called it a night because Erica had to work in the morning.

She headed toward her bedroom, calling over her shoulder. "You know where everything is, help yourself. I'm getting into the shower. My bed is calling my name."

"Thank you, Erica, for everything you've done for me. You're a great friend." As she closed the door, I remembered something I forgot to discuss with her. "Erica," I yelled.

The door came swinging back open as she poked her head out.

"Yeah?"

"Don't tell Tony I'm at your place, please. I'm not ready to face him yet," I pleaded with my friend.

I could see the disappointment in her eyes, but she agreed. "Sure thing."

She closed her door, and I grabbed my bag from the recliner, then headed down the hallway. Making a left toward the spare bedroom, I deposited my bag on the floor, then climbed into bed. I laid staring at the ceiling as I contemplated exactly what to do about Tony. I was so utterly and irrevocably in love with my boss.

CHAPTER NINETEEN

I should've stopped her. Instead, I was standing in the exact same spot when I let the best thing that has ever happened to me walk right out of the fucking door.

"She didn't even give me a fucking chance to explain. She just goddamn assumed I was sticking my dick in any and everything," I growled.

I rubbed my bald head, unsure, for the first time in probably forever, about what to do. I rushed from the room because all I could smell was Remi. Every inch of this bedroom reminded me of her. I grabbed her purse she'd left behind and the bag with her laptop. I called the front desk, making them aware I'd be checking out. I instructed the clerk to have someone box Remi's clothes I purchased for her, as well as mine, and send them to my home in New York.

I clinched the box with the diamond necklace and matching earrings I gave her on our first night here, and my chest tightened. "She's really gone," I muttered as I stepped into the elevator.

A text went out to my pilot to have everything ready for my

arrival in a few minutes. On my way to the airport, I immediately dialed Ashley. I gotta have some clarity on this to help me make sense of it all. I was so thankful she picked up on the first ring.

"Surprised to hear from you," she exclaimed, not bothering to say hello, just forged right on through. I had to smile. It was good to hear a friendly voice.

The weakest laugh I'd ever heard escaped me, despite my current pain. *Damn, this hurt.* "And why wouldn't I call you. I always call you when I'm out of town."

I got into the car waiting for me. "Take me to the airport," I instructed the driver.

The partition went up between my driver and me, reminding me that just an hour ago, Remi and I were making love in this car. My thoughts pushed her away. I refused to acknowledge how my chest was hurting. My heart was crushed from being stepped on. *What the hell am I doing?* This was unlike me, all this pity and feeling sorry for myself. I was fucking Tony St. Clair.

"Wait, why are you going to the airport?" Ashley interrupted my thoughts with curiosity lacing her voice. "I thought you weren't coming back until Sunday."

"Things changed." That was all I could manage to get out. I was irate, hurt, and confused.

"Uh oh, that doesn't sound good. From the social media and news pictures, you seem as if you're having the time of your life."

Her cackling came clearly through the receiver. Ashley always put a smile on my face. This was the worst moment of my life, and she managed to pull one out of me.

Resting my head on the back of the seat, where do I even start? We were having a glorious time, the most fun I'd ever had in my life, until that fucking question. Fucking media.

"She left." I'd never cried over a woman in my life, but I loved Remi, and her not being here with me was bringing me to tears. I took several deep breaths, waiting for Ashley's response.

"What happened?"

I told her everything. By the time I'd reached the actual reason she'd turned tail and ran, I was getting out of my car with Remi's things and onto my private jet.

"When we got back from the aquarium, the media was everywhere in the lobby waiting on us. Someone leaked where we were staying, I guess." I took a deep breath before continuing, "They were just doing what the media does. I'm used to it, but Remi is different. She was uncomfortable when we were being photographed on Riverwalk. I was trying to get her to the elevator as quickly as I could so she wouldn't have to go through that again. Then this asshole yells out something about me having a secret baby or some shit."

A gasp rang out over the line as I settled into the seat for take-off. "Oh, no! And she's pissed."

Remi wasn't pissed, more like distraught.

"Ashley, I've never seen a woman so deflated. When I barged into the room, she was packing her bag. I'm pissed because she didn't give me a chance to tell my side. She just assumed everything was true."

Resting my head against the headrest, I massaged my temples, trying to ease the pain from an oncoming headache.

"You love her?"

Tipping my head as if Ashley could see me, "I love her," I finally choked out.

Tears swelled in my eyes, and I didn't even try to hold them back. I was a broken man. Ashley didn't console me nor interrupt. She just let me get my anguish out until a blanket of calm fell over me and under control.

"So, what are you going to do?"

That's a good-ass question. To be honest, I didn't know. I hadn't planned that far ahead because I couldn't wrap my head around the fact that she'd just left without at least discussing it. I didn't even know where to start.

"Your guess is as good as mine. When I figure it out, I'll call you."

We said our goodbyes, and I promised to at least text her when I landed. I was so fucking tired and could barely keep my eyes open. This entire thing had taken a toll on me. I unhooked my seatbelt and made my way to the bedroom, thankful the chef Remi hired was preparing dinner for me. Food was a brilliant distraction from my heartache and was better than drinking myself into a pitiful stupor. I removed my boots and T-shirt, then lay flat on my back, gazing up at the ceiling. As memories of the time Remi and I spent together flashed through my mind, I quietly drifted off to sleep.

As soon as I landed in New York, I went straight to my house in New Rochelle. My choice to live outside the city was because I wanted to raise a family one day. I wanted my children to grow up differently from me. Granted, I didn't grow up poor. We had just enough, but when I got the chance to leave my old neighborhood, I did with no regrets. Got my parents out too.

I was successful, one of the richest men in America, and owned one of the biggest technological conglomerates in the world. I really did love this house, although it was enormous for one person with its five bedrooms and three baths. I always had plans for a family, just never found the right person. But as I sat in my big ass living room in front of my big ass fireplace, I would give all this shit up to have Remi back. Although I should be upset with her for not giving me the chance to set the record straight, I could see where she was coming from because she did previously walk in on me fucking someone.

I never denied I was a playboy and had fucked many women. But I only loved her and no one else. I quickly dialed the one person who had the kind of contacts I needed for this. I could call Sean, but I needed it done quickly. I needed lines tapped and knew Sean may not be able to or want to. He followed the law to the letter. My disgust on the back burner, I dialed Steve.

"Well, to what do I owe this pleasure?"

The fucker really grated my nerves.

"I need your help with something." Getting straight to the point. I didn't have time for niceties.

"Oh really? Please, do tell. I can't wait to hear this," he goaded.

My teeth ground, sounding in my ears, that was how much I disliked this guy, but I needed his help. I took a deep breath. "I need for you to find out who has been talking to the press about me. Who this woman is that claims she has my child."

A grunt came from the other end of the line. "I understand. Men like us are always targets," he surmised.

"Let's be clear, Steve. I am nothing like you. But you have the connections I need right now."

I debated telling him everything. I didn't want to give him any more leverage over me than this phone call.

"Be that as it may, you came to me, St. Clair. Now, what do I get out of this deal?" I knew it was coming, and I was prepared for it. "I'll give you stock in my company."

A deep chortle peeled out over the line. "Well, this *must* be serious if you are willing to give me stock in your company."

His smugness had me clenching my fists to the point I was sure there would be indentations in the palms of my hands. If we were in the same room, I'd punch him in his fucking mouth.

"More important than you know."

Focused on getting Remi back, I didn't have time to search for who's trying to sabotage my life. If I had to stoop to Smith's level, then I would.

"I'll see what I can do," he agreed and hung up.

Now, with that out of the way, I could concentrate on Remi. I glanced at the time on my cell. *Almost eleven p.m. She's probably asleep.* "When I see her at work, I'll make her sit down and listen to me," I mumbled as I made my way up the stairs to my bedroom.

I was drained from all the emotions consuming me. I'd never let them make my decisions before. It was not the way to do good business, and was not the way I lived my life. I shucked off my clothes, turned off my phone, and climbed into bed as I drifted off into a fitful sleep.

Six a.m. came way too damn early for me. I'd always been a morning person, but not today. I barely wanted to get out of bed, but I made myself. My body was like lead as I dragged my enormous frame to my bathroom. I thought about how Remi loved the tub in our penthouse bathroom, as I stared at mine. Smiling, I thought of how she would really love this one, too.

Without even knowing, the house I'd built for myself and future family had Remi stamped all over it.

"I'm fucking losing it," I mumbled as I took a quick shower.

I didn't want to linger at home because I needed to get to work and talk to Remi before we started our day. I wanted to tell her I was sorry, that I loved her, and that I was investigating where the rumors came from. It was hard for me to even fucking say it or think it. I'd never had sex with anyone without protection until Remi. She's the only woman I wanted. Nothing was going to change my mind.

Walking into my building, early arrivers greeted me as I made my way to my office. It was only seven thirty, and our workday didn't officially start until eight. For the last four years, Remi came to my office every day to go through my daily calendar. She was efficient, well organized, and I relied on her to get me through my workday.

How did I even get by without her? Powering on my

computer, I checked my watch. Remi usually arrived just after eight a.m., so I had a few minutes to check my email and settle myself before I saw her again. All I wanted was for this mess to be cleared up so we could get on with our "happily ever after."

Immersed in checking and responding to emails, I realized it was almost nine, and I hadn't talked to or seen Remi at all this morning. Buzzing her office, I let it ring three times before her beautiful voice told me she was not in the office and to leave a message for her to return as soon as possible.

When I hung up, I decided to check her office. "Maybe she's just busy," I rationalized, heading down the short hallway between our offices. Knocking several times, there was no answer. I put my ear to the door, listening for any movement before I opened it, even though I knew what I'd find. But I still needed to see it before my brain could fully register, she was not here.

Unlike myself, I went into panic mode. Keeping my head under pressure was something I prided myself on. I had no other choice in my line of work and the amount of money I was worth. But right now, none of that mattered because I was fucking losing it. I called her, letting it ring three times. When she didn't answer. I called again, letting it ring four more times. *Maybe she's still asleep.* "Still no answer," I said, heading to HR.

Texted her, she didn't respond. When she didn't, I sent one more. "I fucking hope she didn't quit," I lamented, slipping the phone back into my pocket.

For the first time in my life, I wished that pushing the lobby button made the elevator move faster. After several agonizing minutes, I reached the lobby and made my way to HR.

Mitchell stumbled over himself when he saw me come through the door. "Mr. St. Clair," he stuttered. "What are you doing here?" His voice elevated to a shrill, higher than any man's voice should. It would almost be comical if I wasn't on the verge of hysteria.

I charged toward his desk, causing the man to rear back in his seat away from my opposing stature. "Remi McMillan." I growled her name between clenched teeth, trying to get a hold of myself. "Did she call in this morning? Did she quit?"

My breathing was harsh. I admit, I probably looked like a madman. While Mitchell attacked his database, I focused on calming down. I closed my eyes, just for a second, to get a hold on myself. When I felt like me again, I opened them.

"No, no…no, sir, she didn't call in or quit," he informed me still looking skittish.

"Do you want me to call her, sir?"

My head was throbbing; I massaged my temples to ease some of the pressure before I answered.

My hand dragged down my face, trying to wipe away my fear of the possibility of not seeing her every day. "No, Mitchell, I've called. Can you email me her address, please? Thank you."

I didn't wait for his reply. I turned and went back to my office.

The day waned on and became the longest of my life. Normally, my office was my place of solace. I engrossed myself in my work, enjoying every moment of growing my business and feeling overjoyed because I'd accomplished something. But today, I had no peace. I didn't want to check emails, go to meetings, make or receive conference calls. I didn't want to do anything. My sight wandered to the clock on the wall or the watch on my wrist the entire day. I constantly checked my phone for her response to my texts I had been sending her throughout the day.

ME

Remi, please can you just text me back and let me know you're okay?

Remi, please don't quit on me. On us.

I'm sorry. I love you.

It was a bit excessive and completely out of character for me to send multiple texts begging, but I didn't give a fuck. I'd never lost anything before. Losing my money and my company wouldn't even compare to what I'd lose now. I eyed the address I'd printed out lying on my desk and had been debating, since Mitchell sent it over, on what to do.

When Remi didn't respond to my last text, there was no more debating. I called for my car to meet me to take me home so I could drive myself to see her. My car was more inconspicuous than a limo pulling up to her apartment building. As soon as I was home, I jumped into my black SUV, putting her address in my GPS. Ironically, we only lived forty-five minutes apart, and I never even knew it.

The drive was quick, and when I arrived, I put the car in park, cutting the engine, snatching the keys and stuffing them in my pocket before sprinting toward the gate, barely remembering to lock the doors. I charged up to the gate and buzzed her apartment number. *Nothing.* I buzzed it several more times before I gave up. Returning to my car, I drove my depressed ass home.

CHAPTER TWENTY

Around five in the evening, I decided to roll out of bed. All night I cried, while dodging calls and texts from Mark, until sleep found me. My mind and my body were exhausted from the emotional turmoil. I decided to take a quick shower before Erica got home and talked shit about me wallowing in self-pity. I missed Tony so much I could barely breathe. But I didn't want to be caught up in drama like I was with Mark. I steeled myself, confident of my decision to walk away from Tony. He had a kid, and I didn't want to be a part of any baby mama drama.

I made my way to the shower, relishing the feel of the water beating down on my skin. I kept it brief because if I lingered, my mind would drift back to our nights together, and that was the last thing I wanted to do. Once I finished, I dressed in the lounging clothes Erica let me borrow until my clothes were cleaned. I made my way to the kitchen to get something to eat from Erica's freezer stocked with TV dinners. How in the world she survived on those things, was beyond me. From the fridge, I grabbed a canned soda, popped the top, and poured the contents into a glass until there was nothing left in the can. Remembering

I still had to call my father, I retrieved my phone while I waited for my dinner to finish. I dreaded unlocking it because of what I would see, but I had to know for certain if my father gave Mark my number.

The screen lit up, and several text messages came through. *Ding* after *ding* reverberated through the kitchen. I didn't even bother to read them. There are at least ten missed calls, however, not all of them were from Mark. Several of them were from Tony. Right now, I couldn't deal with him either. I needed to handle just one thing at a time.

First, my father, dialing his number, I waited while his ringtone blasted on the line. I couldn't help but sing along. *You're a shining star, no matter who you are…shining star for you to see what your life can truly be.* I danced my way to the microwave, waiting for my dad to answer his phone, singing the line twice more before his raspy voice came on the line.

"Hello?" He sounded like he was asleep or something.

"Daddy, it's me, Remi. Wake up."

A yawn came across the line. "Hey, baby girl. How are you?"

"I'm good. Daddy, when are you gonna change that ringtone? Earth, Wind and Fire? Really?"

His rich laughter tickled my ear, and I smiled because I loved his laugh. Since Mama died, he had done little of it willingly. "What do you mean? It's a classic! I can't deal with the mess you kids listen to nowadays."

Daddy had always been emphatic that music today had no substance, just a good beat.

I laughed along with him. "Yeah, yeah, yeah. So you say."

"So, what's up, baby girl? Everything all right?"

The worry in his voice was easy to detect, and I wished I could appease him, but I couldn't right now.

"No, Daddy. It's not okay. I don't mean to worry you, and I promise, everything is going well with my job, but," I took a deep breath and blew it out, "Daddy, did you give Mark my number?"

There was no hesitation in his answer, reassuring me that Mark most definitely lied about his intentions to my father. "Of course, I did. He called the other day asking for your number. He said he missed you, and he wanted to get back together with you. I never understood why you dumped him," he ended.

I could literally see in my head the disappointment on his face because I heard its presence in his voice. I'd never told Daddy why we split up. I just didn't want him to be disappointed, but I guess not telling him, had the same result.

"Daddy, I broke up with Mark because I found out he was cheating. And it wasn't one time either," I forced out. "He had an affair with more than one woman."

Marriage and relationships were sacred to my dad. He was madly in love with my mom, even after her death, and believed his daughter deserved the same kind of love.

"Baby girl, I'm so sorry. I didn't know."

God, I loved my father because he always had my back. "I know, Daddy. It's not your fault."

"No, no. It is my fault. Is he bothering you? Is that why you asked me if I'd given him your number."

I nodded as if he could see me. "Yes, Daddy. He's been harassing me nonstop. And now it's getting worse." I was exasperated with this entire thing, on top of my life falling apart.

"Ahhhh, baby, I'm sorry. Does it have anything to do with this man I keep seeing you with flashing across the TV?"

I didn't want to talk about Tony. Especially since everything was so fresh. I purposely didn't go to work today, just so I wouldn't see him. "Daddy, can we not talk about that, please?"

"Sure, baby girl, just so you know, I'll be here if you need me. And I'm gonna have a talk with Mark."

There was determination in his voice. My dad was an intimidating man, but he was also getting up in age. I didn't want him going anywhere near Mark because his texts were becoming more and more hostile. As I was reading over the messages, when I came to Tony's, I closed them without replying.

One problem at a time.

"Daddy, promise me you'll let me handle it. Don't do anything that'll get yourself hurt."

"Okay, honey, but if you don't, I will," he replied.

"Don't worry, Daddy, I will," I reassured him. "Love you, Daddy. I'll talk to you later."

The TV dinner I nuked was forgotten along with my appetite, but I forced myself to take a bite anyway. As soon as I washed my glass and put it in the rack, Erica strode in and engulfed me in a hug before she pulled back to scrutinize me.

"You just got up, didn't you?"

Inspecting myself, I wondered how she even knew that. Then she tried to smooth my hair down, and I couldn't help but laugh. It was still wet from my shower and all over the place.

"I've been up for about an hour," I said, sticking my tongue out at her like a five-year-old.

I shoved her shoulder, both of us laughing, as I sat on the couch as Erica divulged all the happenings at work today. Which, of course, was about me and Mr. St. Clair.

Rolling my eyes as she continued the conversation, I tried not to worry about people in my business. I mean, I was already all over the media. "People are whispering, and I have to say it's intriguing."

I didn't comment about the goings-on at work. "He texted me." I sighed because truth was, I had fallen for him too. "He said for me not to give up on us, and he apologized."

"Well, that's a start. He should apologize," she stated.

"And he said he loved me."

Erica's eyebrows almost touched her hairline. "What did you say?"

"I haven't responded yet."

Our conversation died when my cell rang once again. I hesitated to answer because I knew it would be one of two men I didn't want to talk to right now. "If you don't answer it, I will." I handed over my phone to her. I could tell by all the curse words spewing from her mouth that it was not Tony, but Mark. "You son of a bitch! I don't know you, but if you call her again, it's your ass," she yelled, hung up the phone and handed it back to me. "Block his fucking number, Remi. You don't have to listen to that garbage."

She was so mad. She was almost panting when she hugged me. "Honestly, I hadn't even thought about blocking it. I've been so wrapped up in Mr. St. Clair the past few days," I responded, shocked I didn't think of doing that before. "But I talked to my dad."

"He gave him the number?"

I dipped my head. "Yeah. Mark lied to him. Told him that he wanted to get back with me. Which he *does*, but Dad thought he was helping me because I never told him why we broke up."

We spent a few more hours talking, although it hurt too much to talk about my life as she retreated to her room to get ready for a night out. I headed to her spare bedroom to lie down. Unconsciously, I played with the charm on the necklace I'd refused to take off because it didn't feel right. It brought me comfort like a calming balm for my soul because even though I loved Tony with all my heart and soul, it hurt to be with him. Thinking about everything that happened yesterday had been exhausting. All I wanted to do was get lost in dreamland, so I pulled back the covers and climbed in. It didn't take long before I was in an exhaustion-induced sleep.

CHAPTER TWENTY-ONE

To be quite frank, I didn't expect to hear from Steve so soon. I tried to make it a point not to work from home, but with Remi still not responding to me, I decided to work a little to take my mind off the hell my life had suddenly become.

When I arrived home from visiting Remi's apartment building, Ashley called, trying to convince me to come out and drown my sorrows. I politely declined, and Ashley respected my wishes to just be alone. I thought about texting or calling Remi again, but I didn't think she'd answer. My love had a stubborn streak, but to me it was one of the things I'd adored most about her. She didn't treat me as if I was nobility and she was a servant. My best option was to get a good night's rest—I could barely keep my eyes open, anyway. I'd try again with Remi tomorrow.

And that was what led me to work this morning. A positive thing was, I didn't have to drag myself from bed. I slept okay, soundly but not dreamlessly. My mind kept replaying our time in Chicago, minus when my world came crumbling down. I was whining, but Remi was everything to me.

She was the first woman to treat me normally—whatever that

meant—she was the first woman to make me smile other than Ashley. She was the first woman I hadn't hidden from the media while out on the town. Hell, I kissed her in front of hundreds of people and let them take pictures of us.

I made my way downstairs to the kitchen where Ira had already started my coffee. No matter how many times I told that woman she's off on the weekends, she always snuck by here to brew my coffee. I smiled while pouring a fresh cup because I'd never caught her in the act to chastise her for it. She slipped in and out. And she only brewed enough for the one cup since she knew I didn't really care for it.

I made my way to my office to start my work. I touched the mouse pad, and my computer came to life. Immediately, I saw an email from Steve.

"Damn, that was fast," I murmured, opening up his email.

> This is the ex. And he's also the one who called the reporter about your kid. He paid the woman when the reporter went to follow up. FYI, there is no kid. The woman admitted to my contact, she doesn't even know you personally, only from the media coverage.

Attached to the email were several photos. One of a woman I'd never seen before claiming to be the mother of my child. The second one of the signed statements from that same woman claiming a man named Mark Garrison paid her to tell a reporter she had a child with me. And the last one of a man about medium height, slight frame with milk chocolate skin, a fade that led into sideburns and full beard standing in front of Remi's building.

With the phone on speaker, I threw it on the bed while I rummaged through my closet for something to slide on. After four rings, the voicemail picked up, and I waited for the beep to leave my message.

An unfamiliar terror rose in my chest as I scanned the picture again. I quickly hit the print button on all the pictures and ran upstairs to call Remi. "Remi," I yelled into the phone. "Remi, please, baby, pick up the phone." I tried to calm my words, hearing the panic in my own voice. "I'm coming over okay. I'll be there in thirty minutes." I hung up and dialed her right back. This time, she picked up. "Oh, thank God," I squeezed out through bated breath, grateful she wasn't hurt or anything.

"What do you want, Mr. St. Clair?" Her use of formality made me wince, but I didn't have time to dwell. I pulled on my shoes. Grabbing the phone, I ran through the kitchen door and into my garage.

"Remi, baby, where are you?" I pleaded.

She recognized the alarm in my voice and answered me. "I'm at my apartment picking up some things, then I'm meeting Erica at the salon."

"Listen to me. I'm on my way there. Don't let anyone in until I get there. Don't open the door, okay?"

I floored my SUV down my driveway, then turned down the street that would take me straight to the highway.

"Tony, you're scaring me what do you...hold on, okay, someone's at the door."

My heart was beating out of my chest. "No, Remi! Don't open the door," I yelled, but she put the phone down despite my pleas.

Her melodious voice was muffled and distant, but there was no mistaking the blood-curdling scream before everything was dead silent. "Remi!" I screamed at the top of my lungs into the phone. "Remi, fucking answer me!"

But it was no use. That son of a bitch had her. I knew he did. And I'd do everything in my power to get her back. I instantly flipped through my contacts, trying to keep my eye on the road, and dialed Steve, the only person who had tabs on this guy.

"Tony." The answer was instantaneous. "Surprised to hear from you."

Maybe it was from the time difference or because I called with questions so quickly, but the shock was apparent in his voice. "Tell me everything you have on this guy, Steve. No bullshit," I growled impatiently, still twenty minutes away from Remi's apartment.

A creak of the bed, then rustling of clothes, maybe he was getting up out of bed. "I'll be back," he responded to someone in the room with him, but it was muffled as if he had covered the microphone. "Give me a minute to get to my study." I drummed my fingers on the steering wheel as the other gripped it so tight my knuckles turned white. Paper crackled from his end. "Okay, let me see. From the information we gathered, Mark Garrison comes from a well-to-do family in Charlotte, not mine or your status of course, but he has money," he added. "Attaches to and then drops women like pieces of paper to be scattered in the wind."

I found the description poetic somehow, but I guaranteed Remi wouldn't be one of those papers. He ticked off several other pieces of information from his list before he interjected, "Longest relationship he's ever had was with your personal assistant," he informed me. To think Remi stayed with that asshole for so long got to me in ways I didn't even comprehend. Fury coursed through me just thinking about him touching what was mine. I couldn't wait to find this guy so I could beat him to a pulp for everything he'd ever done to her.

"The picture you emailed me. Is that man still around? Is he still tailing this guy?" When I turned into the parking lot to Remi's building, I jumped out of my SUV and hopped her gate, certain that was how he got to her without a key card required to get into her building. I slipped through the door as one tenant walked out the door, I made my way up the flight of stairs as quickly as I could. "Is he tailing him!!"

I wouldn't apologize for my forcefulness or tone. Remi's life was in danger, and if I lost her, what would I do?

"I just texted him. He's on him. Has your girl too, but St. Clair, I'm not letting my man get caught up in your mess. He'll stay on him and keep tabs until you get there. That's it."

"Tell him to watch for my black SUV. I'll need his information."

"He'll be in a blacked-out truck. I'll text you his location."

Smith hung up, and I took the steps two at a time up the six flights of stairs. As soon as I got to Remi's apartment, I noticed her door was wide open, and by it, blood was splattered on the floor where her necklace with the key-to-my-heart charm lay carelessly. They'd overturned a chair. There was a broken lamp on the floor, which looked as though it had been thrown against the wall. From the signs of struggle, I could tell my baby fought like hell.

The realization and disgust that she was going through this almost brought me to my knees. If that motherfucker hurt her, I'd kill him. I grabbed Remi's phone from the counter where she left it and slid it into my back pocket. I made my way out of her door and ran into a guy who looked like he might have been a football player. He was as big as I was, but he was meaner looking.

"Did you see anything?" I asked, scrolling through my phone, to call Mitchell. He didn't say anything at first. I pleaded, "Please, she's in danger."

He shook his head. "Her door was open when I got here. I would've stepped in if I had."

I thanked him and ran down the stairs and out of the building, calling Mitchell because he had access to all the employees' personal information. "Mitchell, it's St. Clair. I need you to search a number for me and text it to my phone. Her name is Erica Ryan. I believe she works in development."

I hung up not giving him a chance to respond. The text with

an address from Smith came through. My SUV fishtailed out of the parking lot as soon as I programmed into my GPS. Thank God for modern technology. I'd never been to this side of town before because when I was younger, we stayed out of each other's neighborhoods. As an adult, I basically just kept to myself, so I had no idea where I was going. Going into this neighborhood, I couldn't give two fucks about territory boundaries.

Just as I came to a skidding stop in front of some abandoned apartments, Mitchell came through with Erica's number. I quickly dialed her up. I'd planned to tell her to get the fuck home and wait for me to call her once I had Remi back. She picked up on the second ring. Confusion laced her voice because she didn't recognize mine.

"Erica, it's St. Clair."

There was a pause on the line, and then anger ensued in her every word. "What the hell do you want?"

I smirked at the loyalty she showed her friend, even though I was her boss too.

"Never mind that, Erica. I need for you to get home now. Don't come out until I call you back. And call the police. Tell them someone broke into Remi's apartment," I rushed through.

I didn't mean to alarm her, but I didn't have time for her to get hysterical right now.

Her voice shrilled as she comprehended my instructions. "What do you mean? What's happened?"

She was Remi's best friend. The least I could do was tell her what was happening, but this call was wasting my time. "Erica, I can't go into detail," I rumbled, "but Remi is in trouble. I promise you, though, I've got her."

Without giving her the opportunity to question me, I hung up. Hopefully, she would just do what I asked. I surveyed my surroundings as I gathered my thoughts on how to help Remi.

Back in the day some big corporations started buying up land rights from under the tenants, claiming they would build it up and make it into a shopping hub. Basically, gentrification that went unfulfilled for one reason or another. I opened my glove compartment and retrieved my gun, cocking it to ensure a bullet was in the chamber. With the safety on, I made my way out of my SUV, stuffing it in my waistband at my back. I waited as a blacked-out truck slowly approached and parked. Out stepped an enormous man dressed in all black with a bald head.

I offered my hand, which he rejected. "They are in the last apartment on the right on the third floor. He has a gun, but I didn't see anyone else with him," he reported, then got back in his truck and drove away.

"Awkward, but efficient," I muttered before turning off my phone and placing it on the floor of my SUV.

I pulled Remi's necklace out of my pocket, whispering a prayer and kissing it before pushing it back down in my pocket. I made my way as quietly and steadily as I could, hoping I didn't let on I was coming. The whole time I was taking the stairs two at a time, I was praying these old stairs didn't creak and give me away. At first, I could only make out mumbling. But the closer I came to the apartment he had her in, the louder the yelling became.

"You fucked him, didn't you!" I heard a man, whom I assumed to be Mark, scream. I withdrew my gun from the waistband.

"Fuck you, Mark! What I do or who I fuck is none of your business!" Remi yelled back.

A smack echoed through the hallway. A low chuckle, followed by an all-out laugh rang clear throughout the old building. Remi was baiting this fucker. Why? I tried my damnedest not to rush in before I assessed what was happening. I continued my steady creep, listening intently.

"I'm so fucking glad I got out when I did," she announced.

"You think I'm going to sit by and watch my woman trounce around the world with some guy because he has money? The fuck I will." His voice was low and menacing, convincing me he would very well hurt her if I didn't do something.

There was no door to the apartment. When I approached it, I quickly peeked in and out. He held a gun on Remi, but she didn't seem afraid. Her chin was held high, and she stared that fucker right in the eyes, with her hands cuffed behind her back and her lip bleeding. His handprint was visible on her cheek despite her hazelnut skin. When I took a second look, her neck was bruised, and both her eyes were blackened. My blood was boiling, but it wasn't going to do Remi any good if I didn't calm down. I took two deep breaths before my gigantic frame stepped out into the open.

CHAPTER TWENTY-TWO

The creak in the hallway had me raising my head and putting me on full alert. Although both my eyes were sure to be black, only one of my eyes was swollen shut. I could see out of the other. It landed on the most beautiful man I'd ever seen. But relief quickly turned to panic when I realized Tony was in danger.

"No leave!" I screamed at him.

I didn't want him here. Not with Mark being so unpredictable. Mark whirled the gun from me to our unexpected guest. Tony was standing there with both hands raised high. A gun held in one. He didn't move but tried to assure Mark he was not there to hurt him.

"Man, I'm good. I'm not here to hurt you. I just want you to let Remi go." Tony bent slowly toward the floor, putting his gun down. I could see the gun in Mark's hand tremble as he trained it on Tony. My mind raced as I tried to figure out how to get out of the cuffs Mark had around my wrists. My gaze moved back to Tony who subtly shook his head while his eyes pleaded to me not to make any rash moves.

"What the hell are you doing here? I'm not letting her go. She's coming back with me," Mark yelled.

Mark needed to keep talking while I came up with a plan. I didn't want him shooting Tony because of me.

"I'm not going anywhere with you, Mark. Are you even listening to yourself right now?" My outburst caused him to divert his attention away from Tony.

His focus was momentarily off Tony and back on me. I could see the indecision as he tried to figure out which of us was the bigger threat.

"I couldn't stand seeing you with him." He pointed the gun back at Tony. "You are mine, Remi."

Trying to rise to my feet, I made it up to my knees. "Why? So, you can just keep cheating on me. The moment you saw me happy, you tried to ruin it," I shouted at him, keeping his attention on me.

Tony moved deathly quietly to Mark's right, and I tried not to follow his movements. Keeping my focus trained on Mark, it looked like he'd been through hell. Mark had always been a big man, but the Mark standing before me had lost at least twenty pounds. His face was ashen and drawn. The man who was once so put together with model good looks, who I gave my heart to, was now a shell of a man. One who I barely recognized.

"What happened to you?" I marveled. My voice just a little above a whisper.

I felt sorry for what he had become.

"Don't worry about—" He didn't have time to finish before chaos ensued.

Tony rammed his shoulder into Mark's stomach while his attention was on me. The gun flew out of Mark's hand and skidded to the other side of the room. While I was still in cuffs, I managed to struggle to my feet and move out of the way of the two behemoths wrestling on the floor.

When they stopped rolling, Tony was on top of Mark. He

reared his meaty fist back and crashed it into Mark's face over and over until Mark was no longer making any sound or moving. The tears raced down my face, relieved that this unbelievable situation was over. Tony stood and rifled through Mark's pockets.

"What are you looking for?" I made my way carefully to him, wary of Mark lying unconscious on the floor. Tony held the keys to the handcuffs high in the air as he climbed to his feet to unlock me before pulling me into his hulking frame. As I inhaled his scent, I relaxed, and the tears flowed once more. I loved this man so much. I couldn't even imagine what would've happened had he not shown up. "You came for me?" The question came out muffled because I buried my face in his chest.

"I'll always come for you."

He kissed me on the top of my head and pulled me out of the apartment to his truck before my world went black.

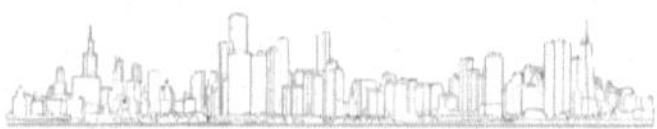

The bright lights when I awakened, had me squinting trying to clear my vision. When I raised my hand, there was some resistance. I glanced at my left hand to see a tube coming out of it as the steady *beep, beep, beep* of the machine recording my heartbeat became clear.

My head turned to the left and slumped in the chair was Tony. I took the time to peruse his body as he slumbered. He wore a simple navy T-shirt with a white logo, that was hard to make out. His jeans hugged just enough of his powerful legs, and his feet were adorned in wheat Timberland boots. He looked just as delicious in street clothes as he did in his designer suits and ties.

For a few more minutes, I watched him sleep. He'd let his beard grow out some, and the hair on his head was showing a little. I noticed a hint of dark circles under his eyes, as if he hadn't been sleeping well.

Did I do this to him?

I was brought out of my reverie when he stretched and yawned. My eyes were drawn to how the stretch showcased his body, causing an immediate wetness between my thighs. He was fully awake. His eyes locked with mine, and my heart melted with the concern I found in his.

He grabbed my hand and brought it to his lips. "How do you feel?

"My mouth is dry," I croaked. "I feel like shit, and my face hurts like hell."

His hand raked through my hair and trailed down my face gently. *How can this giant of a man's touch feel as light as a feather?* I leaned into his touch, absorbing his warmth and strength. After this, I was sure I needed it. Not only do I feel his strength, but his anger, too.

I kissed his palm, trying to calm the beast. "Can I have some water, please?"

The fury in his eyes dissipated slightly as he strived to take care of me, as I hoped it would. He seized the plastic mug with the hospital logo on it and a plastic spoon. "No water, just ice chips," came out strangled as he struggled to hold on to his emotions.

I was astonished that this man, *this billionaire*, had genuine feelings for me. He helped me to a sitting position in the bed and fed me ice chips until I was satisfied I wouldn't sound like a frog when I started asking questions.

"What happened to Mark?"

I hoped the police would get there before he escaped.

"On our way to the hospital, you passed out. Erica had called the police. They went to your apartment. Then I called them and gave them the address of where we left Mark. Remi, I have never been so scared of anything in my entire life. I thought I'd lost you."

The sincerity in his voice had me choking back the tears I was on the verge of releasing.

"How long have I been here?"

Just then, the door swung open, hitting the wall, startling both Tony and me. In strolled Hurricane Erica with a visage that almost had me cowering. "An entire day, bitch." With tears in her eyes, she threw herself on the bed, wrapping her arms around me. "Don't you ever do anything like that to me again," she whispered in my ear through her tears. She abruptly stood, pointing her finger at Tony. "And you, Mr. St. Clair, you better be good to her, or I will kick your ass and then quit my job."

Erica turned and left the room just as quickly as she came in, and I couldn't help but laugh at the look on Tony's face as he stared after Hurricane Erica. "Well, I can't have her kicking my ass, now, can I?" He reached into his back pocket and pulled out his phone. He scrolled for a few seconds before handing me the phone. "Read it," he demanded.

I was confused as to what he wanted, but soon realization dawned on me as I read the headline of the article.

St. Clair Baby Proved to be a Lie; Woman was Paid.

My already swollen eyes tried to make out the gist of the article before I handed him back his phone. The tears streamed down my face as he told me how he uncovered who set him up. "Remi, I asked Steven Smith to track down the woman who accused me of having a kid with her," he began. "His search led to Mark Garrison."

"So, Mark paid her?" I reasoned, and he nodded. "How did you find me? I didn't get the chance to say much to you before Mark ambushed me."

I couldn't believe Mark would do all that just to ruin my happiness.

He shared with me the pictures Steve sent over to him. "They took the picture of Mark outside of your apartment. As soon as I realized it, I called you and tried to warn you to leave because I had no clue when it was taken or if he was still in the area." He lifted my hand again and kissed my palm. "God, Remi, I was so scared."

His eyes pooled with tears again, but none trailed down his face. My eyes softened. I loved him with all I had in me. Tony suddenly stood, making his way to a bag nestled in the room's corner. He reached in the bag and pulled out something, but from the angle I was sitting I couldn't see what it was. Whatever it was, he hid behind his back as he slowly made his way back to the bed.

Instead of sitting in the chair he once occupied, he made a comfortable spot on the bed near my knees after I scooted over, making room for him. He handed me a box about the length of my forearm. I already knew exactly what it was. The red whelps on my neck still stung a little from when Mark snatched it from my neck.

I opened it, and to be honest, I expected to see it broken in two, but instead it was my platinum necklace, whole again, charm and all. The necklace was laced through the most exquisite ring I'd ever seen.

"Onyx and diamonds," I guessed.

He chuckled, shaking his head. "No, they're white and black diamonds inlaid in platinum," he corrected me.

"Oh, diamonds," I repeated breathlessly, tears streaming down my face.

The ring, with its black diamonds, glinted in the fluorescent lights of the hospital room. Tony pulled the necklace out of the box, unfastened it to pull the ring free. Once he went down on one knee, I fucking lost it. I couldn't stop the tears from streaming down my face even if I wanted to.

"Remi McMillan, I never thought I would find someone who makes me bat-shit crazy and so loved as much as you do. You have been my obsession, my infatuation, since I saw you dance that night in that bar four months ago. I was miserable when you left me and scared out of my mind when I thought," he paused, taking a deep breath, gathering his composure, "he took you. Now that I have you back, I'm not letting you go. Will you please do me the honor of becoming my wife?"

My voice was frozen. Nothing would come out. I didn't want him to think I was turning him down, so I bobbed my head profusely while holding my left hand out for him to slide the ring onto my finger. It was beautiful and unique, just like our journey. He pulled me to him gently, bringing our lips together in a tender caress of love. He reared back, a light kiss on my lips and then the tip of my nose. Before he returned to his seat, he picked up the box with my necklace in it. "Lift some, love."

I did as he asked, and he clasped the necklace around my neck. I'd missed the weight of the thing, as it laid above my breast. My hand grasped the charm, raking it back and forth across the chain as I smiled at the man who had given me everything.

The excitement in my private room, unable to tell if it was emanating from me or him, had me giddy for the future of our relationship. I was excited, ready to get out of this place.

I began to pull back my sheets and hop down off the bed. "Whoa, what are you doing? You're in here until tomorrow. They want to monitor you overnight," he informed me, trying to help me back into the bed.

My head was swimming, so I didn't argue, even though I wanted to leave. A grin formed on my lips as Tony remained at my side. As my world faded around the edges, I couldn't believe how lucky we were to have found one another. I whispered, "I love you," before my world turned black and sleep claimed me.

"I love you too," a deep bravado echoed in the darkness.

CHAPTER TWENTY-THREE

"Shit, I'm late."

I checked my watch as I made my way down the street to the coffee shop Erica, and I met at almost every morning. But not today. She left earlier this week for a conference in Chicago. It had been a month now since Tony and I made our relationship official. He refused to let me move back into my apartment and had all of my belongings packed and shipped to his home. At first, I argued. We were spending all of our free time with one another, and I wanted my own space, to think, to spend time with Erica, to be individuals until we set a date for the wedding. But going back to my apartment and seeing the damage my fight with Mark caused, not only physically but emotionally as well, I couldn't stay. The sight of my blood broke me, and I sobbed in Tony's arms until my tears subsided. Then, I finally agreed to move in with him.

At first, our mornings were chaotic as we tried going about our individual routines, but now we were in sync as a couple living together. He got up hours before I did so he could get to the office before the employees.

Living with one another helped me learn a lot about Tony and about myself. For example, he made breakfast most mornings when his cleaning lady, Ira, didn't, and he disliked coffee. All those years he was just giving me shit, and when he became interested, it was a way for him to spend more time with me.

I arrived at the shop. The line was moving quickly. I checked my watch again, and it was already five after eight. A month ago, I would have been on the verge of a breakdown being this late, but now I took it for what it was, and I'd get there when I got there. I chuckled at my summation. So much had changed.

With my order filled quickly, I took a sip of my caramel mocha, savoring the chocolaty sweet taste, and walked the two blocks to the St. Clair building. Entering the lobby, I was greeted by nods and waves from some, while others whispered behind their hands, heads close together. But it didn't bother me because I was secure in my relationship with Tony.

I headed straight to my office from the elevator. Dropping the empty coffee cup in the trash, I laid my bag on the floor next to my desk before scooping my planner and pen and straight to Mr. St. Clair's office. I knocked like always and waited for permission to enter—it was hard to break the habit.

"Come in, Remi." His baritone called out to me from the other side of the door. A shiver ran through my body. His voice always had this effect on me. When I entered, his back was to me as he finished up a call and put the phone into his pocket.

I sat in the same chair I always sat in, in front of his desk, waiting patiently to get started with my day. "You're late," he said as he took his seat. A mischievous smirk formed on his lips as I watched the flames enter his eyes. "I guess I'll have to punish you when we get home."

His promise zipped straight to the vertex between my legs, and I was instantly wet. With intensity in his eyes, he rose from his seat. I reared as far back as I could in the chair, trying to get away from him. "What are you doing, Mr. St. Clair?" I asked, not bothering to keep the seduction from my voice.

"I need to kiss you."

He inched himself closer to me, his eyes full of fire as he stared at my lips. Unconsciously, I licked them, ready for him. It was just a light touch, but it was full of love and promise.

He tried to deepen the kiss, but I wrenched away. "Mr. St. Clair, I don't think it's appropriate for us to do this." I loved playing this game. It had become our way of getting one another ready for when we got home. "While we're at work, you're my boss, and I am your assistant. You can't touch me or kiss me," I said in a singsong voice, but my pussy fluttering told a different tale.

His erection was pressing forward, straining for release. I stood abruptly and moved backward as he kept coming forward.

His laughter enveloped me. "So, you giving the orders now? I'll take you right here on my desk."

I was so horny that I almost gave in.

"No, no, no." I repeated the mantra more for me than him.

His laugh rang out again, and I joined him.

He sighed once our laughter quieted. "Okay, but just so you know, I've obsessed about taking you that way for the longest time."

His confession had me thinking of all the fun things we could do when we got home. I was going to head straight to his home office.

"We'll play later," I promised him when I sat back in my seat, shooing him to his.

I opened my planner, ready to start the day, but first I had a little surprise for Mr. St. Clair. I had a little secret I was bursting to share. I gave him a rundown of his day, just as I always did. "You have a meeting at nine and a conference call at ten," I ticked off, trying not to smile as I did.

"Yes, yes, I see it on my calendar. Thanks for that." He had finally decided it was worth his time to check his calendar.

"I added one more thing to it for twelve," I said, no longer able to contain my grin. I watched as he checked his calendar. The brightest light I'd ever seen glistened in his eyes as they locked with mine.

"Is this for real?" he questioned, rising from his desk chair.

I could only bob my head because if I spoke, I knew I would just sob, the tears were already streaming down my cheeks.

He came around his desk, hauling me into his arms. "How long have you known?"

"I just found out this morning, but I had my suspicions," I grinned.

"I'm going to be a father," he whispered and placed the sweetest kiss on my lips.

Our time was just beginning, and the future was brighter than ever. Somehow, my surly billionaire boss had made me one of the happiest women in the world, despite what we'd been through in our pasts, we were happiest together.

EPILOGUE

ONE MONTH LATER

"I'm so glad I didn't have to cancel my trip to Chicago," I relayed to Remi as I packed for my conference.

I'd asked for permission months ago to attend this conference. It was the biggest technological development conference in the US.

"I'm glad you didn't either," she agreed as she held up a dress I threw on my bed where she was sitting.

I snatched it from her and threw it in the suitcase. "What? That's the least hoochiest dress I own." Laughter peeled from my best friend as she helped me pack my toiletry bag. "And I can't believe Mr. St. Clair booked me the penthouse suite. Girl, I'm going to be living it up!"

I couldn't hide the excitement of going on this trip. After what Remi went through, I almost felt guilty for going, but she didn't need me as much since she and Mr. St. Clair were together now. Now, don't get me wrong. I am happy for Remi. She deserved happiness after what she went through.

Remi and I met four years ago at a coffee shop down the street from St. Clair Technologies. I worked in the technology development department, while Remi was Mr. St. Clair's personal assistant.

A few weeks ago, an ex-boyfriend kidnapped Remi and threatened to kill her because her relationship with Mr. St. Clair being plastered all over social media and entertainment news made him jealous as hell. And crazy. It was the only way to describe that whole situation. Thankfully, Mr. St. Clair saved her before she was killed.

I must admit, she seemed happy as I flittered around my room packing for this trip. To be honest, it was beneficial to get away for a while. What happened to Remi shook me, and I haven't been the same since. I almost lost my best friend, and I hadn't been my usual perky, outgoing self because of it. I hoped this trip would be filled with rest and relaxation so I could get back to my old self.

I arrived at the hotel promptly for dinner. The private elevator took me straight to the penthouse. As soon as the doors opened, I dropped my bags and hightailed it to the shower without taking the time to admire the room. Remi had described it to me, anyway. I just wanted to unwind and get back to my fun-loving self. I've missed that girl. Tonight was going to be the start of that.

I noticed a bar when I came in, and I was starving right now. Relieved that the festivities for the conference started tomorrow morning at ten, I didn't have to worry about getting up too early. I'd decided to wear the dress to dinner Remi turned her nose up at, but I loved it. It was deep purple with off-the-shoulder straps and gathered at the hip, opening into a split. It hugged my curves just the way I liked.

I stepped into it, adjusting the straps so they showed the right amount of shoulder and cleavage. I skipped over to the mirror and combed out my bob, admiring myself. I was hella sexy in this dress. With my curling iron, I bumped my hair a little at the crown of my head and fingered each curl to give my hair some lift.

My simple silver cross and silver diamond studs were my only jewelry tonight, along with light makeup and a dark purple gel gloss to complete the outfit. Sliding on my open-toe heels, I grabbed my purse from the bed and scurried to the elevator.

It was invigorating, being in a new city and meeting unfamiliar people. As soon as I stepped out into the lobby, the atmosphere of this whole place changed. People crowded the lobby in their Sunday best, all looking to have a pleasurable time. The bar, which was becoming crowded quickly, was going to be my safe place tonight. I ordered a sangria and asked for a menu. I liked the fruit in the drink more than the drink itself. Nonetheless, it was a welcome coolant to my dry mouth. The cheerful conversations all around me reminded me of why I loved being around people, the camaraderie, laughter, and genuine friendship.

As soon as my food arrived, I sensed someone watching me. I stopped mid bite of my wings and scanned the surrounding room. When I didn't see anyone, I went back to my food. It was not until a few seconds later that I noticed someone sitting next to me. He had almond-shaped, light brown eyes that popped under black-rimmed glasses and small diamond studs in his ears. I glanced in his direction, then back to my plate. I admit he was fine. His hair was neat, close-cut, faded on the sides, full beard with connecting sideburns and mustache linking to his beard.

"How are you?" he asked, calling one of the two bartenders serving tonight.

I turned to him. "I'm fine. How are you?"

A grin spread across his face revealing stark white, straight teeth. This man was gorgeous, and I could already feel the fire coursing through my veins. "I'm doing well, thanks for asking." He offered his hand to me. At first, I didn't touch it, because I'd been digging in these chicken wings nonstop since they've arrived.

He laughed and offered me a handkerchief from inside of his jacket pocket, bringing attention to how his designer suit jacket fit just right against his muscular frame. I chuckled too. "I'm sorry," I apologized as I took the handkerchief from him and wiped my hands.

Once I was satisfied there was no trace of grease or chicken crumbs, I reached for his still, extended hand. "Martin," he introduced himself, and his baritone went straight to my lady bits.

"Erica." My voice sounded breathless even to my ears. I cleared my throat and tried again. "Erica. Nice to meet you, Martin."

He scooped up his handkerchief, stuffing it back into his suit pocket, which looked to be a Valentino. He had a nice style and expensive tastes. His dark coal shirt was absent a tie and unbuttoned around the neck. It was paired well with the charcoal-gray suit. Martin was the total package from what I could see. And to be honest, I was more than likely gonna choose him to scratch the itch he'd brought on.

"Nice to meet you." Heat from embarrassment swamped my face. He caught me ogling him. It didn't matter. I couldn't wait to see what's under that three-thousand-dollar tailored suit. "I wanted to come over and ask if you would like to join me at my table." He gestured to the empty table in the corner to the right of us.

He appeared to be alone, so I took him up on his offer. He helped me from my barstool, signaling to the bartender to send our drinks to his table. Heat raced up from the small of my back. My body absorbed the warmth of his hand as he led me to his table. He pulled my chair out like a true gentleman, which was something I wasn't used to, and as gracefully as I could, I took my seat.

Our conversation was pleasant, not too personal. "So, Erica, business trip or pleasure?"

I took a sip of my drink. "Business." I didn't offer any other information. "And you?"

"Same." He smirked. I think he'd caught on to my game—that I was not trying to be his friend. I just wanted him in my bed.

After several more drinks, we were laughing as if we were long-lost friends catching up on time missed.

He rose from his seat, offering his hand. "Erica, would you like to dance?"

Hesitation caused me to scan the dance floor because there was no one else in the bar dancing. But then I remembered, this was what I used to do. I was the one who danced until dawn, drank all night, and just had fun. It didn't matter if anyone else was doing it or not. I promised myself, the old Erica was coming back, and she was coming back tonight. So, I threw caution to the wind, accepted his hand, and let him lead me out of my chair to the dance floor.

The man could move. There was no doubt about that. He made me wonder what type of moves he had in bed. For such a well-built guy, he was as graceful as a professional dancer. Hell, for all I knew he was one. Our bodies meld together in courtship. When the music slowed, Martin drew me in close. Crushing me to his body. I didn't object because I'd been expecting the feeling of his hands on me. I most certainly wanted my hands on him.

With no hesitation, I raised my hands to his chest, causing his muscles to tense under my touch. We swayed to the music, in our own bubble as everyone around us faded. He inhaled deeply. Whether it was to dispel his nerves or to take in my scent, I didn't know. He bent at the knee a little, and his beard tickled my neck, then my lips. I stifled a moan. This man stirred my blood like no other had. I wondered what he had in store for me.

His lips moved from my neck to my ear. A pinch elicited another soft whimper from me when he bit my earlobe. I turned toward Martin, placing a sultry kiss upon his luscious lips. He deepened the kiss, tracing the seam of my lips, asking permission to enter. *I did,* and *I didn't* dare hold back from him. If this was the start of the rebirth of Erica, then I was going all out. I kissed Martin back with everything I had. When we finally, reluctantly, pulled apart, we were both panting for breath. His fingers lifted my chin higher, and he placed another light touch to my lips.

He whispered against them. "Come to my room."

I didn't take it as a question, but a demand that left my knees like jelly. My entire body was primed and ready for the fuck of my life. I didn't trust a groan of pleasure not to escape my mouth if I answered him, so I just gave a curt nod. He led me out of the bar, through the lobby to a second private elevator adjacent to the one I'd used. We stepped in, and I was engulfed in his hulking frame. His body molded to mine, and I believed this could be the best night I'd ever had in my life. In the back of my mind, I was screaming…*oh shit. This man could be trouble.*

Keep an eye out for book two
A Billionaire's Love
coming in April 2026!

A LOOK AT BOOK TWO:

A Billionaire's Love

Erica Faulk used to be the fun one... the shots-at-midnight, no-strings-attached, live-out-loud kind of woman.

After her best friend barely survives a violent attack by her ex, Erica's wild lifestyle suddenly feels hollow. On a business trip to Chicago, she's trying to stay focused, stay present, but when she crosses paths with a gorgeous stranger who actually listens, something in her shifts. Martin Wright is warm, grounded, and exactly the kind of good trouble she never saw coming. And with him, she starts to wonder if she's finally ready for more.

What she doesn't know is that Martin is also hiding something, like the fact that he's a billionaire tech entrepreneur trying to escape his high-pressure life. And just as things heat up between them, a mysterious redhead enters the picture, one who wants **Erica** just as much as Martin does. As desire builds and trust wavers, Erica finds herself caught between the safety of old patterns and the risk of something real.

As temptation pulls from every direction, Erica has to ask herself: Is she chasing a new beginning, or running straight into another heartbreak?

AVAILABLE APRIL 2026

ABOUT THE AUTHOR

Tamika Brown (writing as Mika B.), a *USA Today* and Amazon bestselling author, lives in a quiet town in North Carolina with her husband and their three children. When she's not writing,· Tamika loves diving into a good book, binge-watching Ancient Aliens, The Secret of Skinwalker Ranch, and anything Marvel-related. A devoted sports fan, she eagerly awaits the start of every NFL season.

Tamika's stories specialize in growly Alpha shifters, dominant men, and the fierce, passionate women who love them. Her books are a blend of heat, heart, and high-stakes devotion, crafted for readers who crave intensity and romance with bite.

www.ingramcontent.com/pod-product-compliance
Lightning Source LLC
LaVergne TN
LVHW030921080826
845145LV00013B/2994

* 9 7 8 1 9 6 9 8 7 6 2 4 0 *